A
BOY'S RIDE

Gulielma Zollinger

1st WORLD
LIBRARY
Literary Society

A Boy's Ride

Gulielma Zollinger

© 1st World Library – Literary Society, 2005
PO Box 2211
Fairfield, IA 52556
www.1stworldlibrary.org
First Edition

LCCN: 2004195628

Softcover ISBN: 1-4218-0449-2
Hardcover ISBN: 1-4218-0349-6
eBook ISBN: 1-4218-0549-9

Purchase *"A Boy's Ride"*
as a traditional bound book at:
www.1stWorldLibrary.org/purchase.asp?ISBN=1-4218-0449-2

1st World Library Literary Society is a nonprofit
organization dedicated to promoting literacy by:

- Creating a free internet library accessible from any
computer worldwide.
- Hosting writing competitions and offering book
publishing scholarships.

A Boy's Ride
contributed by Tim, Ed & Rodney
in support of
1st World Library Literary Society

CHAPTER I

It was the last of May in the north of England, in the year 1209. A very different England from what any boy of to-day has seen. A chilly east wind was blowing. The trees of the vast forests were all in leaf but the ash trees, and they were unfolding their buds. And along a bridle-path a few miles southwest of York a lad of fourteen was riding, while behind him followed a handsome deerhound. A boy of fourteen, at that age of the world, was an older and more important personage than he is to-day. If he were well-born he had, generally, by this time, served his time as a page and was become an esquire in the train of some noble lord. That this lad had not done so was because his uncle, a prior in whose charge he had been reared since the early death of his parents, had designed him for a priest. Priest, however, he had declined to be, and his uncle had now permitted him to go forth unattended to attach himself as page to some lord, if he could.

To-day he seemed very much at home in the great wood as he glanced about him fearlessly, but so he would have been anywhere. Apparently he was unprotected from assault save by the bow he carried. In reality he wore a shirt of chain mail beneath his doublet, a precaution which he the more willingly took because of his good hope one day to be a knight, when not only the shirt of mail, but the helmet, shield, sword, and lance would be his as well.

It was not far from noon when he came to the great open place cleared of all timber and undergrowth which announced the presence of a castle. And looking up, he saw the flag of the De Aldithelys flying from its turrets.

There was a rustle in the thicket, horse and deerhound pricked up their ears, and then ran pursued by flying arrows. And now ride! ride, my brave boy, and seek shelter within the walls! For till thou reach them, thy shirt of mail must be thy salvation.

The drawbridge was yet down, for a small party of men-at-arms had just been admitted, and across it rushed boy, and horse, and dog before the warder had time to wind his horn: the horse and rider unharmed, but the deerhound wounded.

The warder stared upon the strange boy, and the boy stared back at him. And then the warder crossed himself. "'Tis some witchcraft," he muttered. "Here cometh the young lord, and all the time I know that the young lord is safe within the walls."

The grooms also crossed themselves before they drew up the bridge. But the boy, unconcerned, rode on across the outer court and passed into the inner one followed by the wounded dog. Here the men-at-arms were dismounting, horses were neighing, and grooms running about. The boy, too, dismounted, and bent anxiously over his dog.

Presently a young voice demanded, "Whence comest thou?"

The boy looked up to see his counterpart, the son of the lord of the castle, standing imperiously before him.

"From York," answered the stranger, briefly. "Hast thou a leech that can care for my dog? See how he bleeds."

"Oh, ay," was the answer. "But how came he wounded? He hath been deer-stealing, perchance, and the ranger hath discovered him."

"Nay," replied the strange lad, in tones the echo of his questioner's. "Thou doest Fleetfoot wrong. We were but pursuing our way when from yonder thicket to the north and adjoining the open, a flight of arrows came. I had been sped myself but for my shirt of mail."

The leech had now advanced and was caring skilfully for the dog while the strange lad looked on, now and then laying a caressing hand on the hound's head.

Meanwhile the men-at-arms conferred together and exchanged wise looks while a stout and clumsy Saxon serving-man of about forty shook his head. "I did dream of an earthquake no longer ago than night before last," he said, "which is a dream that doth ever warn the dreamer and all concerned with him to be cautious and careful. Here cometh riding the twin of our young lord: and the Evil One only knoweth how this stranger hath the nose, the eyes, the mouth, the complexion, the gait, the size, and the voice of our young lord, Josceline De Aldithely. Thinkest thou not, William Lorimer, it were cautious and careful to put him and his hound outside the walls, to say nothing of his horse?"

William Lorimer, the captain of the men-at-arms, smiled in derision. A great belief in dreams and omens was abroad in the land: and nowhere had it a more devoted adherent than in Humphrey, the Saxon serving-man, and nowhere a greater scoffer than in William Lorimer.

"I see thou scoffest, William Lorimer," pursued Humphrey. "But were he put out, then might those minions of the king shoot at him once more, and spare to shoot at our young lord. I will away to our lady, and see what she ordereth."

There had always been times in England when no man who stood in the way of another was safe, but these were the times when women and children were not safe. For perhaps the wickedest king who ever sat upon the English throne occupied it now, and his name was John.

This king had tried to snatch the kingdom from his brother, Richard Coeur de Lion, and had failed. When Richard was dead, and John was made king in his stead, there was still another claimant to the throne, - his nephew Arthur, - and him the king in 1204 had murdered, so report said, with his own hand. This was the deed that lost him Normandy and all his other French possessions, and shut him up to rule in England alone. And the English soon had enough of him. He was now in a conflict with the Pope, who had commanded him to receive Stephen Langton as Archbishop of Canterbury. This John had refused to do. Now, the kingdom, on account of the king's disobedience, was under the papal interdict, and the king was threatened with excommunication.

England had at this time many, many churches, and their bells, before this unfortunate situation, had seemed to be ringing all day long. They rang to call the people to the ordinary church services; they rang to call them to work, and to bid them cease from work. They rang when a baby was born, and when there was a death. And for many other things they rang. Now, under the interdict, no bell rang. There were no usual church services, and everywhere was fasting. A strange England it seemed.

The king had never gotten on well with his barons, and they hated him. Nevertheless they would have stood by him if he had been at all just to them. And surely he needed them to stand by him, for all the world was against him. The French were eager to fight him, and the Church was arrayed against him. But all these things only made the king harder and more unjust to the barons because just now they were the only ones in his power, and his wicked heart was full of rage. He had hit upon one means of punishing them which they all could feel, - he struck them through their wives and children. Some of the barons were obliged to flee from England for their lives. Many were obliged to give the king their sons as pledges of their loyalty. In every man's knowledge was the sad case of one baron who had been obliged to flee with his wife and son into hiding. The king, through his officers, had pursued them, ferreted them out of their hiding-place, taken the wife and son captive, shut them up in prison, and starved them to death. Lord De Aldithely himself had been obliged to flee, but his son would never be delivered up peaceably to the king's messengers, for De Aldithely castle was strong and well defended.

This was the meaning of the arrows shot at the strange

boy. The king's messengers, who were constantly spying on the castle from the wood in the hope of gaining possession of the person of the young lord by stratagem, had taken him for Josceline, the young heir of the De Aldithelys.

And now came a summons for both lads to come to the ladies' bower, for Humphrey had not been idle.

"My change of raiment?" said the strange lad, inquiringly.

"Shall be in thy chamber presently," answered Josceline.

"I would that Fleetfoot also might be conveyed thither," said the stranger, with an engaging smile.

"It shall be done," promised Josceline.

He gave the necessary commands to two grooms, and the lads, each the counterpart of the other, waited a few moments and then started toward the tower stairway, followed by the grooms bearing the huge dog between them on a stretcher. The stair was steep, narrow, and winding, and built of stone. Josceline went first, and was followed by the stranger, who every now and then glanced back to speak a reassuring word to his dog. At the entrance to the ladies' bower Josceline paused. "Thou mayest, if thou like, lay the dog for a while on a skin by my mother's fire," he said, and looked inquiringly at his guest.

"That would I be glad to do," was the grateful reply. "See how he shivers from the loss of blood and the chill air."

For answer Josceline waved his hand toward his mother's parlor, and the grooms, conveying the dog, obediently entered. For all but Humphrey, the Saxon serving-man, were accustomed to obey the young heir unquestioningly. But Humphrey obeyed no one without question. It was often necessary to convince his rather slow reason and his active and many superstitions before his obedience could be secured. No one else in the castle would have dared to take his course, but Humphrey was thus favored and trusted because he was born a servant in Lord De Aldithely's father's house, and was ten years older than the mistress of the castle, whose master was now gone. He had already told Lady De Aldithely all that he knew of the strange lad, and had advised her, with his accustomed frankness, to put lad, horse, and hound at once without the castle walls. Lady De Aldithely had listened, and when he had finished, without any comment, she had commanded him to send the two lads to her.

For a moment Humphrey had seemed disappointed. Then recovering himself he had made answer, "Oh, ay. It will no doubt be best to see for yourself first, and there is no denying that the three can then be put outside the walls."

Receiving no reply, he had withdrawn and delivered his message.

Lady De Aldithely was standing evidently in deep thought when the little group entered. The strange lad looked at her curiously. He saw a slight figure clad in a green robe, and as she turned he caught the gleam of a jewel in the golden fillet that bound her wimple on the forehead. Her eyes were blue, and her look one of high courage shadowed somewhat by an expression of anxiety. One could well believe that, however anxious and worried she might be, she would still dare to do what seemed to her best. She now diligently and eagerly compared the two lads, glancing quickly from one to the other, and their exceeding great likeness to each other seemed to strike her with astonishment. At last she smiled and spoke to the stranger. "Thou art welcome, my lad," she said kindly. "But whence comest thou? and what is thy name?"

"I am to-day from York, and I am called Hugo Aungerville," was the frank reply with an answering smile.

"To-day," repeated Lady De Aldithely. "That argueth that thy residence is not there, as doth also thy name, which is strange to me."

"Thou art right," replied Hugo. "I come from beyond Durham, from the priory of St. Wilfrid, the prior whereof is my uncle, I having no other kin so near as he."

"And whither dost thou journey?" asked Lady De Aldithely.

"South," was the answer. "My uncle, the prior, would have had me bred a priest, but I would be a knight. Therefore he hath at last given me his blessing and bid me fare forth to attach myself to the train of some nobleman."

"Why did he not secure thee a place himself?" asked Lady De Aldithely in surprise.

"Because he hath too great caution," was the answer. "These be troublous times. Few be true to the king, and no man knoweth who those few be. Should he choose for me a place and use his influence to secure it, perchance the next week the noble lord might be fleeing, and all in his service, under the hatred of the king. And there might be those who would say, 'Here is Hugo Aungerville, the page to my lord, and the nephew of the prior of St. Wilfrid.' And then might the king pull down the priory about my uncle's ears, - that is, I mean he would set my uncle packing. For the priory is fat, and with the prior gone - why, the king is so much the richer. Thou knowest the king."

"Too well," rejoined Lady De Aldithely, with a sigh. "The Archbishop of York is 'gone packing,' as thou sayest, and the king is all the richer therefor. And this is thy dog that hath the arrow wound," she continued, as she advanced a few steps and laid her hand on the hound's head. "I have here a medicament of wonderful power." She turned to a little casket on a table and unlocked it. Then taking out a small flask, she opened it and, stooping over the dog, poured a few drops on the bandage of his wound. "He is now as good as well," she said smilingly. "That is, with our good leech's care, which he shall have. Nay, thou needst not speak thy thanks. They are written in thy face. I see thou lovest thy dog."

"Yea, my lady, right well. I have naught else to love."

"Except thine uncle, the prior," said Lady De Aldithely.

"Except my uncle," agreed Hugo.

All this time Josceline had waited with impatience and he now spoke. "He is not to be put outside the walls, mother, is he?"

"Nay, my son. That were poor hospitality. He may bide here so long as he likes."

CHAPTER II

Life was rather monotonous at the castle, as Hugo found. Occasionally the men-at-arms sallied out, but there were no guests, for Lady De Aldithely was determined to keep her son, if possible, and would trust few strangers. It was a mystery to Humphrey why she had trusted Hugo.

"I may have dreams of earthquakes," he grumbled, "and what doth it count? Naught. Here cometh a lad, most like sent by the Evil One, and he is taken in, and housed and fed, and his hound leeched; and he goeth often to my lady's bower to chat with her; and often into the tilt-yard to practise with our young lord Josceline; and often lieth on the rushes in the great hall at the evening time before the fire with the men-at-arms; and he goeth to the gates with the warder and the grooms; and on the walls with William Lorimer; and Robert Sadler followeth him about to have speech with him and to hear what he will say; and he is as good as if he were My Lord Hugo with everybody, when he is but Hugo, a strange lad, and no lord at all."

It was as Humphrey had said. Hugo was a favorite with all in the castle. His company was a great solace to Lady De Aldithely in particular. She was drawn to trust him, and every day confided more and more to him concerning her painful and perilous situation. "I am convinced," she said one day when two weeks had passed, "that there is mischief brewing. I fear that I shall lose my boy, and it will break his father's heart."

Hugo looked sympathetic.

"Thou knowest that fathers' hearts can break," she said. "Our first King Henry fell senseless when his son was lost."

"What fearest thou, Lady De Aldithely?" asked Hugo.

"Treachery," was the answer. "There is some one within the castle walls who will ere long betray us."

Hugo was silent a while. He was old for his years, very daring, and fond of adventure. And he loved Lady De Aldithely not only for her kindness to him, but for the attention she had given to Fleetfoot. At last he spoke. "I have a plan. But, perchance, thou mistakest and there is no traitor within the walls."

Lady De Aldithely looked at him quickly. "Nay, I am not mistaken," she said.

"Then this is my plan," announced Hugo. "Josceline and I be alike. I will personate him. In a week Fleetfoot will be quite recovered. We will go forth. They who watch will think they see Josceline and pursue me. I will lead them a merry chase, I warrant thee."

"But, my boy!" cried Lady De Aldithely. "What wild plan is this? Thou lead such evil men a merry chase? Speak rather of the dove leading the hawk a merry chase."

"Even so I will lead them," declared Hugo. "If they catch me, they shall do well."

Lady De Aldithely smiled at the boyish presumption. "My poor lad!" she said. "How if they catch thee with an arrow as they caught Fleetfoot? Thou mightest find no castle then to give thee shelter, no leech to salve thy wound."

"For thee, because of thy kindness, I will risk that," declared Hugo, after a pause.

Lady De Aldithely put up her hand. "Hush!" she said. "Speak no more at present to me, and nothing on the subject at any time to any but me. I hear footsteps."

The footsteps, bounding and light, drew nearer, and presently Josceline looked in at the door. "Come, Hugo!" he cried. "Let us away to the tilt-yard and do our exercise."

Josceline was already an esquire, and very diligent in the exercises required of an esquire as a part of his training for knighthood. But not more diligent than Hugo had been during his stay at the castle. For Hugo felt himself at a disadvantage on account of having been bred up at the priory, and was eager to make up for his shortcomings. In all their practice Robert Sadler, one of the men-at-arms, was present. And both boys liked him very well. He was not a young man, being some sixty years old, and gray and withered. He was of Irish parentage, and short in stature; and he had a tongue to which falsehood was not so much a stranger as the truth. He was also as inquisitive as a magpie, and ready to put his own ignorant construction on all that he saw and heard. The two boys, however, had never stopped to think of his character. He was always praising their performances in the tilt-yard, and always deferring to them, so that they regarded him very favorably and were quite ready to abide by his judgment. To-day he was waiting for them with a tall horse which he held by the bridle. "I would fain see both of you vault over him," he said.

Josceline advanced, put one hand on the saddlebow and the other on the horse's neck, and vaulted over fairly well. After him came Hugo, whose performance was about equal to Josceline's.

"It was the cousin to the king that could not do so well as that," commented Robert Sadler.

"And how knowest thou that?" asked Josceline, complacently. "Didst thou see him?"

"See him!" exclaimed Robert Sadler. "I have seen him more times than thou art years old. And never did he do so well as thou and Hugo."

With hearts full of pride the two went from vaulting over the horse to striking heavy blows with a battle axe.

"Ah!" cried Robert Sadler. "Could the cousin to the king see the strokes that ye make, he were fit to die from shame. He can strike not much better than a baby. I could wish that all mine enemies might strike me no more heavily than the cousin to the king."

"This cousin to the king must be worthless," observed Josceline, his face red from the exertion of striking.

"Worthless!" exclaimed Robert Sadler. "It were not well that the king heard that word, but a true word it is. Worthless he is."

"I knew not that the king had a cousin," observed Hugo, with uplifted axe.

"There was never a man born," declared Robert Sadler, recklessly, "who had not a cousin. And would the king that hath everything else be lacking in a common thing like a cousin? Thy speech is well nigh treasonable. But strike thou on. I will not stay to see thee put the king's cousin to shame, and then hear thee deny there is such a one." And he stalked off to the stables leading the horse.

"I fear thou hast angered him," said Josceline. "But no matter. He will not harbor anger long." And so it proved. For before the two had finished striking he had returned to the tilt-yard apparently full of good humor.

Two days went by. Then Lady De Aldithely spoke again to Hugo of his project. "Hast abandoned thy plan?" she asked.

"Nay, my lady," he replied. "How should I abandon it? Is it not a good one?"

"Good for my son," admitted Lady De Aldithely, "but bad for thee."

"Thou wilt find it will be bad for neither," said Hugo, stoutly. "I am resolved."

Lady De Aldithely sighed in relief. "Come nearer," she said. "I would confide in thee, and none but thou must hear. I have discovered the traitor within our walls. For a sum of money he will deliver my son to the king. Ask me not how. I have discovered it."

Hugo looked at her and his eyes flashed indignation. "Deliver Josceline, he shall not!" he cried.

"He could but for thee, for we are powerless."

"Then again I say, he shall not."

"Come nearer still," said Lady De Aldithely. "I would tell thee the man's name. What sayest thou to Robert Sadler?"

Hugo stared. "Robert Sadler!" he repeated. "Why, 'tis he of all the men-at-arms, save William Lorimer, who is kindest to Josceline and me. He will be ever with us; in the tilt-yard, in the stables, in the hall, everywhere."

"To watch you," said Lady De Aldithely. "To mark what you say. To catch your plans."

"He shall catch no more plans from me!" cried Hugo, indignantly. "I will speak no more with him, nor be with him."

"Ah, but thou must," counselled Lady De Aldithely. "Wert thou to turn from him, as thou sayest, he would know at once thou hadst been warned against him, and would hasten his own plans. What said he to thee yesterday?"

"He did ask me when I should leave the castle."

Lady De Aldithely's face clouded with anxiety. "And

what didst thou answer?" she asked.

"I said it might be one day and it might be another. For thou didst forbid me to speak of my plan."

"I marvel at thy prudence," smiled Lady De Aldithely. "Where didst thou learn it?"

"From my uncle, the prior. He never telleth aught to any man. And no one can wring from him ay or nay by a question."

"A blessing upon him!" breathed Lady De Aldithely.

The boy's eyes brightened. "He is a good man, my uncle, the prior," he said. "And ever he saith to me, 'In troublous times a prudent tongue is worth ten lances and shields.'"

Lady De Aldithely smiled. "May he keep his priory in peace," she said. "'Twere a pity that he should lose it."

Hugo looked at her gratefully. Not every one so leniently regarded the prior's prudence. In more than one quarter his reticence was severely blamed. By some it was called cowardice, by others self-seeking.

"And now thou knowest the worst," said Lady De Aldithely. "Within three days I will contrive to send Robert Sadler hence on an errand. When he is gone thou shalt go forth in the daylight, and that same night my son and I will flee into Scotland. There, if no one tracks our steps, we may be safe. Were I to drive Robert Sadler forth as a traitor, I know full well that some other would arise in his place to practise treachery against us. And so we flee."

And now Hugo drew himself proudly up. He felt that he was trusted and that he was doing a knight's part in rescuing a lady in distress, though he had not, as yet, taken his knightly vow, and was not even an esquire.

Lady De Aldithely saw it and smiled. "Thou must put off that high look, dear lad," she said. "It might beget wonderment in the brain of Robert Sadler, and so lead him to seek its cause. Look and act as thou hast in the past. Call to mind thine uncle, the prior, and guard not only thy tongue, but the glance of thine eye, and the carriage of thy body."

Hugo blushed. "I fear I am like to mar all without thy counsel," he said humbly.

"Thou art but a lad," replied Lady De Aldithely, kindly, "and my counsel thou shalt freely have. And now I must tell thee that thou art to take our good Humphrey with thee on thy journey."

Hugo started and looked disappointed. But all he said was, "Dost not think him very like an old crone, with his dreams and his omens and his charms?"

"I may not criticise Humphrey thus," said Lady De Aldithely, gravely, "because I know his great faithfulness to me and mine. And thou knowest there is much superstition abroad in the land - too much to make it just to single out Humphrey for dislike because he is tainted with it. I send him with thee because I have the highest regard for thy safety. Thou wilt consent to take him to attend thee?"

"If thou require it," answered Hugo, reluctantly.

"I do require it," said Lady De Aldithely, "and I thank thee for yielding. Now go. Come not again to me until Robert Sadler be well sped on his journey. Had I but known that he was treacherous and greedy of gold, no matter how gained, he had never been admitted to these walls."

Obediently Hugo left the apartment and slowly descended the winding stair. And almost at the small door of the stairway tower he found Robert Sadler waiting for him. The traitor was growing impatient and was now resolved to proceed more boldly. "Thou stayest long with her ladyship," he began. "I had thought the sun would set or ever thou came down the stair."

Hugo did not meet his glance. He was trying hard to conceal the sudden aversion he had to the man-at-arms, the sudden desire he felt to look him scornfully in the face, and then turn on his heel and leave him. And he knew he must succeed in his effort or Josceline was lost.

Meanwhile the man-at-arms stole questioning glances at him. He could see that the boy was not his usual self, but he did not guess the cause of his changed manner. With his usual prying way he began:

"Thou hast been here now a fortnight and more. Perchance her ladyship will be rid of thee. Was't of that she spake to thee?"

And now Hugo had sufficiently conquered himself so that he dared to lift his eyes. Innocently he looked into the traitor's face. "We spake of my uncle, the prior," he said.

For a moment Robert Sadler was silent. "That is it," he thought. "She will send him packing back to his uncle. The lad wishes not to go. Therefore he looks down. Now is the time to ask him about the postern key. When one is angered a little then is when he telleth what he hath discovered."

He cast a searching look at Hugo, but by it he learned nothing. The boy now began to take his way toward the tilt-yard, and Robert Sadler kept close at his side, talking as he went.

"Women be by nature suspicious, you will find," he began. "They be ever thinking some one will be breaking in; and ever for having some one on guard. Her ladyship now - surely thou knowest she keepeth the postern key herself, and will trust no one with it. The grooms and the warder at the great gate she will trust, but it is the postern she feareth, because she thinketh an enemy might be secretly admitted there. Knowest thou where she keepeth the key? I would but know in case my lord returneth suddenly, and, perchance, pursued, since the king will have his head or ever he cometh to his home, he hath such an enmity against him. And all because my lord spake freely on the murder of Arthur and other like matters. He might be sped to his death awaiting the opening of the postern while her ladyship was coming with the key."

"Cometh the lord soon, then?" asked Hugo, interestedly.

"That no man can tell," answered Robert Sadler. "He is now safe over sea in France; but he might be lured back if he knew the young lord Josceline was in peril."

"In peril, sayest thou?" asked Hugo. He was learning his lesson of self-control fast.

"Why else are we mewed up here in the castle?" demanded the man-at-arms. "I be weary of so much mewing-up. If the king will have our young lord Josceline to keep in his hand so that he may thereby muzzle his father, why, he is king. And he must have his will. Sooner or later he will have it. Why, who can stand against the king?"

"And how can that muzzle his father?" asked Hugo.

"Why, if Lord De Aldithely, who is a great soldier, and a great help to victory wherever he fighteth, should join with King Louis of France to fight against our king - why, then it would go ill with Josceline if he were biding in the king's hand. And, knowing this, his father would forbear to fight, and so be muzzled."

"And Josceline would not otherwise be harmed?" asked Hugo.

"Why, no man knoweth that," admitted the man-at-arms. "The rage of the king against all who have offended him is now fierce, and he stoppeth at nothing."

"I know not so much as some of such matters," observed Hugo, quietly.

"Nor needest thou," answered the man-at-arms. "It is sufficient for such as be of thy tender years to know the whereabouts of the postern key. I would ask the young lord Josceline, but, merry as he is, he turneth haughty if one ask what he termeth a meddling question. He would say, 'What hast thou to do with the whereabouts of the postern key?' And then he would away to his mother with a tale of me, and the key would be more securely hidden than before."

"And Lord De Aldithely still further endangered if he came riding and pursued?"

"Even so. I see that thou art a clever lad. Much cleverer than thy years warrant. And I warn thee, speak to no one of what I have said to thee, or it may be worse for thee. But tell me plainly, since we have gone so far, knowest thou the whereabouts of the key?"

"Nay," answered Hugo. "I know not. I have never before thought of the postern and its key."

The traitor's frowning face cleared. "I believe thou speakest truly," he said. "Thou art so full of being a knight that thou thinkest only of knightly exercises in the tilt-yard. I will speak a good word for thee, and it may be thou wilt be admitted a page to the Earl of Hertford."

"And hast thou influence there?" inquired Hugo, with assumed interest.

"Yea, that have I," answered Robert Sadler, falsely. For he had no influence anywhere. "I will so speak for thee that thou wilt be page but a short while before thou art made an esquire. Do thou but bide quiet concerning what hath passed between us, and thou shalt fare never the worse."

Then he departed to the stables and Hugo was left alone. To be able to conceal what one feels is a great accomplishment. Rarely do people of any age succeed in doing so, and it was with a feeling of exultation over his success that the boy looked after Robert Sadler.

The next day Lady De Aldithely summoned her men-at-arms before her in the castle hall. She had a missive in her hand. "I must send one of you on a journey," she said. "More than one I cannot now spare to go to Chester. Who will take this missive from me to the town of Chester, and bring back from my aunt what it calleth for?"

A light flashed in the eyes of Robert Sadler which Lady De Aldithely affected not to see. The opportunity he had been seeking was before him. He would go out alone, but he would not return alone. When the drawbridge should be lowered to admit him on his return the king's messengers with a troop of horse would be at hand. They would make a rush while he held parley with the old warder. They would gain entrance to the castle; Josceline would be taken, and the reward for his own treachery would be gained. He had plenty of time to think of all this, for the men were slow to offer. Aside from Robert Sadler they were all true and devoted adherents of the De Aldithelys, and each one imagined the castle and its inmates safer because of his presence. Therefore none desired to go.

"No man seemeth willing to do thy ladyship's behest," said Robert Sadler, with a crafty smile. "I will, by thy leave, undertake it."

Lady De Aldithely looked calmly upon him. "Thou shalt do so, Robert Sadler," she said courteously, "and thou hast my thanks for the service. Thou shalt depart to-morrow morn, and thou shouldest return by the evening of this day week. See that thou bringest safely with thee what the missive calleth for."

"I will return at eventide of this day week," promised the traitor as he received the missive.

"And now," he said to himself, when Lady De Aldithely had retired from the hall, "let her keep the postern key. I care not for it."

CHAPTER III

It was now mid-June. The air was dry and cool. But Robert Sadler thought not of June nor dryness and coolness of air as in triumph he made ready for his journey.

"I should have gone," grumbled Humphrey the serving-man when he heard of it. "Who knoweth this Robert Sadler? My lord had him at the recommendation of Lord Clifford and he hath been at the castle not yet a year. Who knoweth that he is to be trusted? I should have gone. I did dream of serpents last night, and that foretelleth a prison. Robert Sadler will no doubt be caught by some marauding baron as he cometh again from Chester, and he will be thrown into the dungeon, and then my lady will see."

So grumbling he was summoned to the ladies' bower just as the drawbridge was lowered to permit the departure of Robert Sadler. Ungraciously he obeyed; and just as ungraciously he continued his grumbling in her ladyship's presence. "I did dream of serpents last night," he began, "and that foretelleth a prison."

Lady De Aldithely shivered. "I pray thee, speak not of prisons, Humphrey," she said firmly, "but attend my words."

"Am I not faithful?" demanded Humphrey.

"Thou art, my good Humphrey," was the reply.

"Was it then for Robert Sadler to do thine errand?"

"I have a greater errand for thee," was the grave answer. "Robert Sadler is a traitor, and we have much to do ere he return."

Humphrey seemed bewildered. "And wouldst thou trust a traitor?" he at length demanded.

"Abroad, good Humphrey, and in a small matter, but not within these walls."

The dense Humphrey showing still by his countenance that he could not comprehend his mistress, Lady De Aldithely spoke more plainly. "I must tell thee, Humphrey, that Robert Sadler designeth for a sum of money to deliver Josceline to the king."

Humphrey stared.

"I have discovered it, and have been almost crazed in consequence. But a deliverer hath come."

"I saw no one," said Humphrey in a dazed tone.

"Didst thou not see Hugo?" asked Lady De Aldithely with a faint smile. "My lord will be fain to do much for him when he heareth what Hugo will do for Josceline."

"And what can a lad like him do?" demanded Humphrey. "Thou hadst better trust me. I am forty years of age and have served the De Aldithelys all my life."

"I do trust thee, Humphrey, and I do honor thee by sending thee to attend on this brave lad, Hugo."

"I will not go," declared Humphrey. "Why should I leave thee and Josceline to serve a stranger? Here I bide where my lord left me."

"Wilt thou not go at my command, Humphrey?"

There was no reply but a mutinous look, and Lady De Aldithely continued, "Thou hast doubtless seen how very like in appearance Hugo is to my son. This good lad, Hugo, this best of lads, Hugo, will, for my sake and Josceline's, assume to be my son. He will ride forth toward London as if he made to escape to his father in France. The servants of the king will hear of it through the spies they keep in the wood near us. They will pursue him while Josceline and I escape into Scotland."

Humphrey reflected. "I see it, I see it," he said at last. "Hugo is the good lad."

"He is indeed, Humphrey. So good I cannot see him go unattended. Thou art the trustiest servant I have; and so I send thee with him to keep him from what peril thou mayest, and to defend him in what thou canst not ward off. Thou must serve him as thou wouldst Josceline, on pain of my displeasure."

"I did dream of serpents," said Humphrey, slowly, "and they foretell a prison. It were better for thee to abide here, for, perchance, it is not to foretell the fate of Robert Sadler but the fate of Josceline that the dream was sent."

"Abide here, and let Robert Sadler take my son? Nay, good Humphrey, we must away. Hugo and thou to-morrow morn, Josceline and I to-morrow night." And then Humphrey was dismissed with the command, "Send Hugo to me."

Almost immediately the boy appeared, and Lady De Aldithely met him with a smile. "I send thee forth to-morrow morn," she said, "and Humphrey will go with thee - if thou be still of a mind to go."

"I am still of a mind to go, Lady De Aldithely," was the answer.

"Thou knowest the danger to thyself," she said. "And 'twere not to save my only son, I could not let thee take such peril. Cross thou to France, I charge thee, and take this favor to my husband. Tell him, because thou wouldst do knightly service for me and mine, I give it thee. Thou wilt not go unrewarded." And she held out a knot of blue ribbon.

The boy looked from it to her green robe, and back again. Lady De Aldithely saw the look. "Green is not my color, Hugo," she said. "It is but the fashion of the time." Suddenly she drew back her hand and laid the knot against her sleeve. "See how the colors war," she said. "But not more than truth and constancy with the wickedness of this most wicked reign." Then she held out the knot of blue to him again. "Receive it, dear lad," she said. "Whatever knightly service it is thine to render after thou hast taken thy vow, thou canst render none greater than thou dost now render to Matilda De Aldithely."

"And what service is that?" inquired Josceline as he came smiling into the room. "And what solemn manner is this, my mother? There must be great deeds afoot to warrant it." And he glanced from one to the other.

"Thou hast well come, my son," returned his mother, gravely. "I would this moment have sent to summon thee. Thou and I must away to-morrow night to wander through the forest of Galtus and on into the wilds of Scotland, where we may, perchance, find safety."

At this Josceline stared in astonishment. "We be safe here in the castle," he said at length.

"Nay, my son," returned his mother. "Here be we not safe. I had told thee before of the treachery of Robert Sadler but for thy hasty, impetuous nature which, by knowing, would have marred my plans. Thou wouldst have dealt with him according to his deserts - "

"Ay, that would I," interrupted Josceline, "if he be a traitor. And that will I when he returneth."

Lady De Aldithely looked at him sadly. "We be in the midst of grave perils, my son," she said. "Control thyself. It is not always safe to deal with traitors according to their deserts, and never was it less safe than now. When Robert Sadler returneth we must be far away."

But Josceline was hard to convince. "Here is the castle," he said, "than which none is stronger, and here be good men and true to defend it. Moreover, Robert Sadler is now outside the walls. Thou canst, if thou wilt, keep him out, and we have naught to fear. Why should we go wandering with our all on the backs of sumpter mules, and with only a few men-at-arms and serving-men to bear us company?"

"My son," said Lady De Aldithely, rising from her seat, "thy father gave thee into my keeping. And thou didst promise him upon thine honor to obey me. Thou mayest not break thy pledged word."

"I had not pledged it," rejoined Josceline, sulkily, "had I known of wanderings through forest and wild."

"Better forest and wild than the king's dungeon, my son," replied Lady De Aldithely. "We go hence to-morrow night."

During this conversation Hugo had stood a silent and unwilling listener. Josceline now turned to him. "And whither goest thou, Hugo?" he asked. "With us?"

"Nay, let me speak," said Lady De Aldithely, holding up her hand to check Hugo's reply. "Hugo goeth south toward London clad in thy bravery, and with Humphrey to attend him."

Again Josceline showed astonishment. "I understand not thy riddles," he said at last petulantly.

"He is thy counterpart, my son, and he will personate thee," said Lady De Aldithely. "He setteth out to-morrow morn. The king's spies will pursue him, and thus we shall be able to flee unseen."

"And thou hast planned all this without a word to me?" cried Josceline, angrily. "But for my pledged word I would not stir. Nay, not even if I knew Robert Sadler would give me up to the king's messengers."

Lady De Aldithely gave Hugo a sign to leave the room. When he was gone she herself withdrew, and Josceline was left alone in the ladies' bower, where he stamped about in great irritation for a while. But he could not retain his anger long. Insensibly it faded away, and he found visions of wood and wild taking its place.

Meanwhile Lady De Aldithely had gone to the castle hall, when she sent a summons to William Lorimer to attend her there. To him, when he arrived, she unfolded Robert Sadler's treachery and her own meditated flight with her son.

"Thee," she said, "I leave in charge of these bare walls to deal with Robert Sadler on his return. Whatever happeneth I hold thee blameless. Do as seemeth thee best, and when thou art through here, repair with the others I leave behind, to my lord in France. And if thou shouldst ever find Hugo to be in need, what thou doest for him thou doest for my lord and me."

The man-at-arms bowed low. "I will deal with Robert Sadler as I may," he answered. "Only do thou leave me the postern key. As for Hugo, I will not fail him if ever in my presence or hearing he hath need."

Then Lady De Aldithely with a relieved smile gave him the postern key and he withdrew.

The day was now drawing to a close, and an air of solemnity was upon the castle. Each man knew he was facing death; each man was anxious for the safety of Lady Aldithely and her son; and each man cast a sober eye on Hugo and Humphrey. The effect upon Hugo was visibly depressing, while upon Humphrey it was irritating.

Humphrey had been thinking: and while he would be ostensibly Hugo's servant, he had decided that he would be in reality the master of the expedition. "I like not this obeying of strangers," he said to himself. "Moreover, it is not seemly that any other lad than our own young lord should rule over a man of my years. Let the lad Hugo think I follow him. He shall find he will follow me. And why should these men-at-arms look at us both as if we went out to become food for crows? Did I not dream of acorns last night, and in my dream did I not eat one? And what doth that betoken but that I shall gradually rise to riches and honor? Let the men-at-arms look to themselves. They will have need of all their eyes when that rascal Robert Sadler cometh galloping again to the castle with the king's minions at his back."

Now all this grumbling was not done in idleness. For all the time Humphrey was busy filling certain bags which were to be swung across the haunches of the horses he and Hugo were to ride. Brawn, meal for cakes, grain for the horses, and various other sundries did Humphrey stow away in the bags which were to supply their need at such times as, on account of pursuit, they would not dare to venture inside a town. "And what care I that the interdict forbiddeth us meat as if we were in Lent," grumbled Humphrey as he packed the brawn. "Were the king a good king, meat would be our portion as in other years. Since he is the bad king he is, I will e'en eat the brawn and any other meat to be had. And upon the head of the king be the sin of it, if sin there be."

And the packing finished, he went early to rest.

The castle stood on a ridge near the river Wharfe, from which stream the castle moat derived its water. Its postern gate was toward the east, the great gate being on the northwest. From the postern Hugo and Humphrey were to set out and follow along down the river toward Selby. They were to make no effort at concealment on this first stage of their journey which might, therefore, possibly be the most dangerous part of it. They had little to fear, however, from arrows, as the king's men would not so much wish to injure the supposed Josceline as to capture him. They had shot at him before simply to disable him before he could reach the shelter of the castle.

But Humphrey was not thinking of the dangers of the way. He was up and looking at the sky at the early dawn. "I did hear owls whooping in the night before I slept, which foretelleth a fair day for the beginning of our enterprise," he said. "The sky doth not now look it, but my trust is in owls. I will call Hugo. It is not meet that he should slumber now."

Hugo was not easily roused. He had slept ill: for as night had come down upon him in the castle for the last time, he had not felt quite so sure of being able to lead his pursuers a merry chase. And it was midnight when he fell into an uneasy sleep which became heavy as morning dawned. Humphrey knew nothing of this, however, nor would he have cared if he had. By his own arguing of the case in his mind, he was now firm in the conviction that Hugo had been put into his charge, and he was quite determined to control him in all things. So he routed him from his slumbers and his bed without the slightest compunction, bidding him make haste that they might take advantage of the fair day prognosticated by the owls.

This duty done, Humphrey betook himself to the walls near the postern where he had before noticed William Lorimer apparently deeply engaged in reconnoitring and planning. Now, whatever Humphrey lacked, it was not curiosity; and he was speedily beside the man-at-arms, who impatiently, in his heart, wished him elsewhere.

"What seest thou?" began Humphrey curiously as he gazed about him on all sides.

"The same that thou seest, no doubt," retorted William Lorimer, gruffly.

"Why, then," observed Humphrey, slowly, "thou seest what I and thou have seen these many times, - a bare open place beyond the ditch, and then the wood. I had thought some king's man must have shown himself from his hiding."

"Not so, good Humphrey, not so," rejoined William Lorimer more pleasantly as he reflected that he would soon be rid of the prying serving-man. "Hugo and thou will see king's men before I do."

"Ah, trust me," boasted Humphrey, complacently. "I shall know how to manage when we see them."

"Thou manage?" said William Lorimer, teasingly. "Bethink thee, thou art but servant to Hugo. Hast thou not promised Lady De Aldithely to be his servant?"

Humphrey hesitated a moment and then replied: "Yea,

in a measure. But I take it that there are servants and servants. Besides, I did dream of acorns of late and of eating one of them, which doth foretell that I shall gradually rise to riches and honor; and surely the first step in such a rise is the managing of Hugo. My dream hath it, thou seest, that Hugo shall obey me. Wherefore I said I shall know how to manage when I see the king's men."

"Hath Hugo heard of this fine dream?" inquired William Lorimer with pretended gravity.

"Not he. Why should he hear of it? He is as headstrong as our young lord Josceline, though not so haughty. I shall but oppose the weight of my years and experience against him at every turn, and thou shalt see I shall prevail." So saying, Humphrey, with an air of great self-satisfaction, turned and descended the wall to the court-yard.

For a moment William Lorimer smiled. "I would I might follow the two," he said. "There will be fine arguments between them."

CHAPTER IV

The spies who kept watch on De Aldithely castle were four in number, and were hired by Sir Thomas De Lany, who had been commissioned by the king to capture Josceline in any manner that he could. It chanced that there was but one of them on duty in the wood that morning - a certain short, stalky little fellow whose name was Walter Skinner, and who was fond of speaking of himself as a king's man. Formed by nature to make very little impression on the beholder, it was his practice to eke out what he lacked in importance by boasting, by taking on mysterious airs, and by dropping hints as to his connection with great personages and his knowledge of their plans. He was about the age of Humphrey, and though he was but a spy hired by Sir Thomas, he persisted in regarding himself as of great consequence and directly in the employ of the king. He was mounted in the top of a very tall tree in the edge of the wood, and he could hardly believe his eyes when, about nine o'clock, he saw Hugo and Humphrey issue from the postern gate, cross the bridge over the moat, and ride away into the wood, which they struck a quarter of a mile south of him.

In great haste he began to come down the tree, muttering as he did so. "They must all away yesterday morn to York on a holiday," he cried, "and here am I left to take the young lord in my own person. When I have done so I warrant they get none of the reward. I will sue to the king, and we shall see if he who catcheth the game is not entitled to the reward."

By this time he was on the ground and strutting finely as he hurried about for his horse. "A plague upon the beast!" he cried. "He hath slipped halter and strayed. I had come up with the young lord while I seek my horse."

It was some ten minutes before the animal was discovered quietly browsing and brought back to the watch-tree, and then a sign must be made on the tree to let his companions know whither he had gone, so that they might follow immediately on their return. And all this delay was fatal to his catching up with the fugitives. For, once in the wood, Humphrey's authority asserted itself. He pushed his horse ahead of Hugo's and led the way directly through the thick forest for a short distance when he emerged into a narrow and evidently little used bridle-path. "It is well thou hast me to lead thee," he observed complacently. "There be not many that know this path."

Meanwhile Richard Wood, one of the other spies, had unexpectedly returned, read the sign on the watch-tree, and followed his companion. It was at this moment that Hugo discovered that Fleetfoot was not with them. In the excitement of getting under cover of the forest he had not noticed the dog's absence. "Where is Fleetfoot?" he asked as he stood in his stirrups and looked about him anxiously.

"Fleetfoot is at the castle," replied Humphrey, calmly.

"By thy command?" asked Hugo, quickly.

"Ay," replied Humphrey. "Why, what young lord would journey about with a great dog like that in his train? If thou art to play Josceline, thou must play in earnest. Moreover, the hound would get us into trouble with half the keepers of the forest. If ever a deer were missing, would not thy dog bear the blame? So think no more of thy Fleetfoot."

Hugo was silent while the complacent Humphrey jogged on ahead of him. What the serving-man had said was in large measure true. And he thought with a swelling heart that it was not so easy, after all, to personate Josceline when that personating cost him Fleetfoot.

But no less a person than William Lorimer had discovered that Fleetfoot had been left behind. William was fond of both the dog and his master; so now, when Fleetfoot made his appeal to William, the man-at-arms at once responded. He snapped the chain that bound him, and leading him by the collar to the postern gate opened it and let down the bridge. "Why, what would become of thee, Fleetfoot," he said, "when that which is to come to the castle hath come?" Then while the great deerhound looked up expectantly into his face he added as he pointed to the place where Hugo and Humphrey had entered the wood, "After thy master, Fleetfoot! Seek him!"

The deerhound is a dog of marvellous swiftness, and, like an arrow from the bow, Fleetfoot shot across the open space and gained the wood. William Lorimer looked after him. "If thy other commands be no better obeyed, Humphrey, than this which left Fleetfoot behind, I fear thou wilt have cause to lose a part of thy self-satisfaction," he said. Then he drew up the bridge and shut the postern gate.

Hugo had taken the loss of Fleetfoot so quietly that Humphrey with still greater confidence now changed the course slightly, and went down to the river-bank at a point which was half ford and half deep water. But at this Hugo was not so obedient.

"What doest thou, Humphrey?" he demanded. "Was not our course marked out toward Selby? Why wouldst thou cross the river here? We must be seen once on our road, and that thou knowest, or the king's men will not pursue us, and perchance Lady De Aldithely and Josceline shall fare the worse."

"I go not to Selby," declared Humphrey, stubbornly. "And why shouldst thou think we have not been seen? The king's men have eyes, and it was their business to watch the castle."

Then Hugo sat up very straight in his saddle and looked at Humphrey full as haughtily as Josceline himself could have done. "Thou art, for the time, my servant," he said. "And we go to Selby."

For a moment Humphrey was disconcerted, but he did not relinquish his own plan. Presently he said: "If we must go to Selby, let us cross the river here. We can go on the south side of it as well as the north."

Hugo reflected. Then without a word he directed his horse down the bank and into the water, which was here swimming deep. Well satisfied, Humphrey followed.

"I did not dream of acorns and of eating one of them

for nothing," he said to himself. "I shall be master yet."

And hardly had the words passed through his mind when *splash* went a heavy body into the water behind the two swimming horses. Fleetfoot had come up with his master. Swiftly Hugo and Humphrey turned their heads, Hugo with a smile and an encouraging motion of the hand toward his dog, and Humphrey with a frown. "I would I knew who sent the hound after us," grumbled the disgusted serving-man to himself when, the shallow water reached, both riders drew rein for the horses to drink.

Once across the Wharfe Humphrey led the way to a heavy thicket, and dismounting pushed the growth this way and that and so made a passage for the horses, Fleetfoot, Hugo, and himself. In the middle of the thick was a little cleared grassy place where, crowded closely together, all might find room, and here Humphrey announced that they would take their midday rest and meal.

Hugo still said nothing, but he looked very determined, as Humphrey could see. "But I go not to Selby," thought the stubborn serving-man. "I run not my head into the king's noose so near home."

It was an early nooning they had taken, for it was barely half-past twelve when Humphrey broke the silence. He rose, tied each horse securely, and then turning to Hugo said: "Bid the dog stay here. We will go and have a look over the country."

Hugo rose, laid down his bow and arrows, and, bidding the dog watch them, followed Humphrey out of the thicket.

Gulielma Zollinger

The serving-man, who was well acquainted with this part of the country, now made a little detour into a path which he followed a short distance till he came out a quarter of a mile away from the thicket into a grassy glade in the centre of which towered one of those enormous oaks of which there were many in England at this time. "We will climb up," said Humphrey, "and have a look."

Up they went; Hugo nimbly and Humphrey clumsily and slowly, as became his years and experience, as William Lorimer would have said if he had seen him. Barely had they reached complete cover, and the rustling they made had just ceased, when the tramp of two approaching horses was heard. The sky was now overcast with clouds in spite of the prognostications of the owls, and the rain began to descend heavily, so that the two riders sought refuge beneath the tree. Hugo and Humphrey looked at each other and then down upon the horsemen, who were the two spies, Walter Skinner and Richard Wood.

"I had thought to have come up with them ere this," said Walter Skinner. "They had not more than half an hour the start of me."

"Have no fear," replied Richard Wood, who was a tall and determined-looking man. "They have most like gone on to Selby on the north side of the river. We shall catch them there."

"Thou saidst there is no one to watch the castle?" inquired Walter Skinner.

"Ay, I said it," returned Richard Wood. "Why, who should there be when Sir Thomas hath taken the other two and gone off to get a troop together against Robert Sadler's return? There be thirty men-at-arms within the castle, and all will fight to the death if need be, and none more fiercely than William Lorimer. So saith Robert Sadler. He giveth not so brave an account of the warder and the grooms at the drawbridge, for, saith he, 'The warder is old and slow, and the grooms stupid.' It was well we fell in with Robert Sadler as he departed on his journey."

There was a brief silence while the rain still fell heavily, though the sky showed signs of clearing. Then Walter Skinner in his small cracked voice laughed aloud. "The troop will be there, and there will be hard fighting for naught," he said. "For the prize is escaped and we shall capture it and have the reward."

"What thinkest thou of Selby?" asked Humphrey, when the two spies had gone on toward the river.

"I think thou art right," answered Hugo, frankly.

Without a word Humphrey climbed still higher in the tree and gazed after the two till they were hidden from view in the forest.

"Hast thou been before in this wood?" he inquired, when he and Hugo had descended and stood upon the ground.

"Nay," replied Hugo.

"I thought not. Ask me no questions and I will lead thee through it. I know it of old."

Hugo at this looked rather resentful. He had regarded

himself as the important personage on the journey just undertaken, and now it seemed that the serving-man regarded the important personage as Humphrey. And the boy thought that because Humphrey had been right in his purpose to avoid Selby was no reason why he should assume the charge of the expedition. He did not dispute him, however, but followed the triumphant serving-man back to the thicket, to the horses, his bow and arrows, and his dog.

In a short time they were out of the thicket and mounted; and then Humphrey condescendingly said to Hugo: "Follow me, and thou shalt see I will keep out of sight of keepers and rangers. And keep thy hound beside thee, if thou canst. He is like to make us trouble."

At this Hugo felt indignant. He was not accustomed to be treated as if he were a small child.

They now jogged on in silence a few zigzag miles until Humphrey came to another thicket, in which he announced they would pass the night. "Had we kept the open path," he observed, "we might have been further along on our journey, if, perchance, we had not been entirely stopped by a ranger or a king's man."

"The two spies went down the Wharfe toward the Ouse and Selby," remarked Hugo.

"Oh, ay," returned Humphrey. "But the king hath many men, and they all know how to do a mischief for which there is no redress. Hadst thou been a Saxon as long as I have been, and that is forty years, thou hadst found it out before this. And now I will make a fire, for the night is chill, and, moreover, I would have a cake of meal for my supper." So saying, he set to work with his flint and soon had a fire in the small open place in the midst of the thicket.

"Hast thou no fear of the ranger?" asked Hugo.

"Not I. This thick is well off his track. I would have no fear of him at any time but for thy dog. Moreover, he is a timid man, and the wood hath many robbers roving around in it. Could he meet us alone with thy dog, there would be trouble. But here I fear him not."

Hugo laid his hand on Fleetfoot's head. "Thou hast no friend in Humphrey," he said in a low tone as he looked into the dog's eyes. Then, while Humphrey baked the oatmeal cake in the coals, Hugo gave the dog as liberal a supper as he could from their scant supply.

"Be not too free," cautioned Humphrey, as he glanced over his shoulder. "We have yet many days to journey ere we reach London if we escape the clutches of the king's men. Could they but look in at the castle now, I warrant they would laugh louder and longer than they did under the big oak."

Hugo glanced around him nervously.

"Tush, boy! what fearest thou?" said Humphrey. "Here be no listeners. Thou knowest this is the hour. I tell thee frankly I had rather be with her ladyship than to lead thee in safety; yea, even though the way lay, as her way doth lie, through that robber-infested forest of Galtus. Hast heard how there be lights shown in York to guide those coming into the town from that wild place?"

"Yea," answered Hugo, briefly.

Humphrey sighed. "There will be somewhat to do on that journey," he said. "A train of sumpter mules carry the clothing, the massy silver dishes, and the rich hangings; and with them go all the serving-men and half the men-at-arms."

"I pray thee, cease thy speech," said Hugo, still more nervously as he looked about him apprehensively in the semi-darkness of the fire-lit enclosure. "Thy prating may mar all."

"Was it for this," demanded Humphrey, "that I did dream of acorns and of eating one of them, which foretelleth, as all men know, a gradual rise to riches and honor, that I should be bid to cease prating by a stranger, and he a mere lad? But I can cease, if it please thee. I had not come with thee but for her ladyship's commands." And in much dudgeon he composed himself to sleep.

As for Hugo, he lay on the grass, his eyes on the glimmering fire, and his ears alert for any sound. But all was still; and he soon fell to picturing the scene at the castle, - Lady De Aldithely and Josceline, mounted for their journey, going out at the postern gate at the head of the train of sumpter mules and attended by the band of serving-men and men-at-arms. And with all his heart he hoped for their safety. He did not wonder at their taking their treasures with them. It was the custom of the time to do so, and was quite as sensible as leaving them behind to be stolen.

The great deerhound blinked his eyes lazily in the firelight and drew, after a while, the lad's thoughts away from the castle. What should he do with Fleetfoot? How should he feed him, and with what? And how should he get him through the town of Ferrybridge near which they now were, and which they must pass through in the morning, unless Humphrey would agree to swim the horses across the Aire above the town and so avoid it?

And now the wood seemed to awake. Owls insisted to the ears of the sleeping Humphrey that the morrow would be a fair day. Leaves rustled in the gentle wind. Far off sounded a wildcat's cry. And with these sounds in his ears Hugo fell asleep.

CHAPTER V

The fire was plentifully renewed, and Humphrey was preparing breakfast when, in the morning, Hugo awoke.

With what seemed to the boy a reckless hand, the serving-man flung Fleetfoot his breakfast. "He may eat his fill if he will," said Humphrey, noting Hugo's expression of surprise. "He hath already so lowered our store that more must be bought."

"And where?" inquired Hugo.

"At Ferrybridge," returned Humphrey, complacently, to Hugo's dismay.

"I had thought best to avoid Ferrybridge," said Hugo. "I would swim the horses across the Aire above the town."

Humphrey seemed to ruminate a short time. Then he put on a look of stupid wisdom. "Let us have breakfast now," he said.

Hugo looked at him impatiently, and wondered how he could ever have found such favor with Lady De Aldithely. But in silence he took the brawn and oat-cake Humphrey gave him. The horses were already feeding, and, despatching his own breakfast with great celerity, Humphrey soon had them ready for the day's journey. Still in silence Hugo mounted, for a glance at the stubborn Humphrey's face told him he might as well hold his peace.

Straight toward the river-bank rode Humphrey, while Hugo and Fleetfoot followed.

"There!" said Humphrey, when they had reached the river's brink. "Seest thou that thick across the stream? Swim thy horse and thy dog across, and bide there in that thick for me. I go to the town to buy supplies. Last night I did have two dreams. I had but gone to sleep when I dreamed I was going up a ladder. Knowest thou what that meaneth?"

"Nay," replied Hugo. "I am not skilled in old woman's lore."

Humphrey frowned. "Thou mayest call it what thou likest," he said, "but dreams be dreams; and this one signifieth honor. I waked only long enough to meditate upon it and fell asleep again, and dreamed I climbed once more the big oak of yesterday. And that meaneth great preferment. Canst thou see now how I have no cause to fear king's men? For what honor could it be to be caught by them? or what preferment to be laid by the heels in the king's dungeon? And canst thou see how it is meet for me to go into the town, and for thee and the hound to swim the river? I warrant thee the king's men, though they fill the streets of Ferrybridge, will be no match for me with such a dream as that."

Then Hugo lost his temper. "Thou art a foolish fellow," he said, "and moreover thou art but my servant. Where is thy prudence of yesterday? I am of a mind to forbid thee to go into the town. But this I tell thee; I know this region by report. We be not so many miles from Pontefract castle. If thou comest not to the thick by noon, Fleetfoot and I journey on southward, and thou mayest overtake us as thou canst."

"I know not if I can come by noon," answered Humphrey, more submissively than he had yet spoken. "Never have I been in Ferrybridge. I know not what supplies I may find."

"Take care thou find not the king's men," said Hugo. "At noon Fleetfoot and I journey on." With that he directed his horse into the water, Fleetfoot followed, and Humphrey was left on the bank.

"Ay," he said to himself, rather ruefully, "thou canst play the master as haughtily as our young lord Josceline himself when it pleaseth thee. But for all that, last night I did go up a ladder and climb a tree. No doubt I shall yet prevail."

Then he galloped off toward the town, where he mingled with the throng of people quite unnoticed in the number, for, in spite of the interdict which forbade amusements of all kinds, a tournament was to be held at Doncaster, and many were on the way to attend it. Since the king scouted the interdict, many of the people braved it also, and the inns were already full. Humphrey was riding slowly along with curious eyes when, in the throng, he caught sight of Walter Skinner, the pompous little spy, who sat up very straight on his horse, and looked fiercely around, as if to warn the people of what they might expect if they unduly jostled him, the king's man. For so he regarded himself, although he was only the hired spy of Sir Thomas De Lany.

"A plague upon my dreams!" thought Humphrey, his native common sense getting the better of his superstition. "I had never ventured my head in this noose but for them. I must now get it out as I can, but that will never be done by noon."

Almost as soon as Humphrey had seen him, Walter Skinner had seen Humphrey, and had recognized both man and horse as the same he had seen from the treetop leaving the castle with Hugo the previous day. Not finding any trace of the two in the neighborhood of Selby, he had come on to Ferrybridge, while his companion, Richard Wood, had gone south by the very way Hugo would start out on at noon. He gave no sign of recognizing Humphrey, however, and Humphrey seemed not to recognize him.

Said Walter Skinner to himself, "I will not alarm him, and the sooner he will lead me to his master."

While Humphrey thought, "I will not seem to see him, and when I can, I give him the slip."

So up and down the narrow streets rode these two, Walter Skinner looking fiercely upon the innocent throng, and Humphrey apparently gazing about him with all a countryman's curiosity. Noon came and Humphrey managed to find a place for himself and horse at an inn. "I may as well eat and drink," he said, "for what profit is it to be going up and down these narrow streets? At every turn is this little cock of a king's man who, though he croweth not with his mouth, doeth so with his looks. I know not for whom he is seeking. Not for me, or he would assail me and capture me and put me to the torture to tell him where Hugo is, for he thinketh Hugo is Josceline, which he is not, but a stranger, and a headstrong one. There is nothing in dreaming of going up a ladder or climbing a tree, if I get not the better of him." And so he betook him to his dinner.

The little spy followed him, and the innkeeper was obliged to make room for him also, which, when Humphrey saw, he changed his opinion as to whom the spy was in search of. "He thinketh," said Humphrey to himself, with sudden enlightenment, "to follow me quietly and so find Hugo."

Humphrey was ever a gross eater, and Walter Skinner watched him with great impatience and dissatisfaction. For Humphrey ate as if no anxiety preyed upon his mind, but as if his whole concern was to make away with all placed before him.

"It may be," reflected Walter Skinner, "that he hath bestowed his master, as he thinketh in safety, in a neighboring abbey or priory. From whence my master will not be long in haling him out. For what careth the king for abbots or priors? And so let him leave off this partridge dance he hath been leading me about the streets." And he scowled upon the apparently unconscious serving-man.

"Ay, let him scowl," thought Humphrey, with his mouth full of savory viands that filled him with satisfaction. "He may do more scowling ere evening if he like. I did go up a ladder and climb a tree last night."

His dinner over, Humphrey went out to the stables, whither Walter Skinner followed him as if to look after the welfare of his own horse, thus confirming Humphrey's suspicion that he had recognized him. And the serving-man at once put on an air of self-confidence and pride in his own wisdom which effectually concealed his anxiety from the watching Walter Skinner. He entered into conversation with the grooms, and let fall, in a loud voice, such a weight of opinions as must have crushed any intelligent mind to consider. And there about the stables he stayed; for the grooms took to him, and evidently regarded him as some new Solomon.

The impatient Walter Skinner listened as long as he could, but seeing, at last, that Humphrey's wisdom was from an unfailing supply, he went back to the inn, after beckoning one of the grooms to him and giving him a piece of money, in return for which, as he pompously instructed him, he was to keep an eye on Humphrey, and on no account to allow him to escape him; at the same time he threw out hints about the king and his wrath if such a thing should happen.

The groom, who was himself a Saxon, and who hated all king's men, listened respectfully, took the coin, said that he had but two eyes, but he would use them to see all that went on before him, and returned to the stables, where he at once told Humphrey what had passed. "I have a hatred to the king and his men," declared the groom.

"And what Saxon hath not?" asked Humphrey. "I have lived forty years, and in all that time the Normans grow worse, and this John is worst of all."

"Perchance thy master is oppressed by him," ventured the groom.

"Perchance he is, and his lady and his son likewise," returned Humphrey.

The groom looked at him. "I ask thee to reveal nothing," he said significantly. "I have but two eyes, and I must use them, as I said, to see, all that goeth on before me. Do thou but ask Eric there to show thee the way out of the town before the curfew ring. He hateth king's men worse even than I. My master will summon me to the house shortly, according to his custom. That will be the time for thee, for I can in no wise see what goeth on behind my back, nor did I promise to do so."

At once Humphrey betook himself to Eric, explained matters so far as he dared, and received the groom's ready promise to guide him out of the town, which he did within an hour, while Walter Skinner sat impatiently waiting for him to reenter the inn from the stables. Eric did more for him also; for he provided him with provender for the horses and abundant provisions for himself, Hugo, and the dog, receiving therefor a good price which he promised to transmit to his master.

"And now," said Humphrey to himself, when he was well quit of the town, "if the time cometh when Saxon as well as Norman hath preferment, my device shall be a ladder and a tree. And may the king's man have a good supper at Ferrybridge and be long in the eating of it."

Straight to the thicket rode Humphrey at a good pace, but he found no Hugo there. "Here is a snarl to be undone!" he cried. "The lad is too headstrong.

Perchance he hath already run into the noose of the other king's man. For who knoweth where he is? And I shall be held to answer for it. This cometh of a man being servant to a boy and a stranger at that. I will away after him." So saying, he rode to the south, giving all habitations of men and walks of forest rangers a wide berth, and hoping sincerely that Hugo before him had done the same. "For the lad," said he, "is in the main a good lad. And how can I face my lady if harm cometh to him? It is no blame to him that he hath not a knack at dreams to help him on his way."

At the last word his horse shied; for out of the undergrowth at the side of the little glade through which he was riding fluttered a partridge, while, after it, floundering through the bushes with a great noise, came Fleetfoot. In vain Humphrey tried to call the dog from his prey. In a twinkling the unhappy bird was in the hound's mouth and Fleetfoot was off again to the thicket to supplement his scant dinner with a bird of his own catching.

"Here be troubles enough!" cried Humphrey. "King's men on our track, and now partridge feathers to set the keepers and rangers after us. Well, I will push through this underbrush to the right. Perchance Hugo rideth in the bridle-path beyond, since it was from that part the dog came. And he shall put the hound in leash. I am resolved on it. I have no mind to have hand or foot lopped off that so a deerhound may have his fill of partridges."

With a frown he pushed through the underbrush. The sun was setting when he emerged into a path and, at a little distance, caught sight of Hugo jogging slowly along and looking warily about him. He dared not signal him by a whistle, so, putting spurs to his loaded horse, he advanced as fast as he was able, and shortly after came up with the lad, his anger at Fleetfoot's trespass rather increased than abated, and, in consequence, with his manner peremptory.

"Into the thick here to the right," he growled, laying his hand on the bridle of Hugo's horse. "The sun is now set, and we go no farther to-night. In this stretch robbers abound, and I have no mind to face three dangers when two be enough."

Hugo looked at him inquiringly.

"Yea, by St. Swithin!" went on the angry serving-man. "King's men and partridge feathers be enough without robbers." And giving Hugo's horse, which he had now headed toward the thicket, a slight cut on the flank with his whip, he drove Hugo before him, much to the boy's indignation. "Thou hast been drinking!" he cried, turning in his saddle. "Strike not my horse again."

They were barely screened from sight when Humphrey, his head turned over his shoulder, held up his hand warningly. A horse was coming on the gallop. A second elapsed, and then Walter Skinner went by. He had discovered Humphrey's flight a half-hour after Eric had led him out of the city, but the grooms had successfully delayed him half an hour longer. Then he had started in pursuit, and had gone thundering along at such a pace that he could hear nothing nor see anything that was not in full view. This new sight of danger at once pacified both Hugo and Humphrey. The boy forgot what he had been pleased to regard as the insubordination of his servant, and Humphrey forgot the anger he had felt against Fleetfoot and his master.

As soon as they dared, they pushed cautiously farther into the thicket, and presently Humphrey dismounted and tied his horse. Here was no grassy spot within enclosing underbrush where comfort might be found. There was such a place not far off, but Humphrey would not go to it. With his knife he set to work clearing a place large enough for the tied horses to lie down in. Cutting every stick into the very ground, he laid the cut brush in an orderly heap, and thus made a bed for himself and Hugo. Then without a word he went out on foot and down to the bank of the Went, peeled a willow, and came back with a long strip of its bark. "Thou wilt tie this to the collar of thy dog," he said." He hath been trespassing, and hath taken a partridge. Should the keeper discover it and us, thy hand or foot, or mine, must pay for it."

"How knowest thou that Fleetfoot did take a partridge?" asked Hugo, with disbelief in his tone.

"I did see him," replied Humphrey. "And noting whence he came, I did find thee, and none too soon."

There was a short silence. Then Hugo said: "A partridge is not much; and, as thou sayest, if thou hadst not seen Fleetfoot, thou hadst not found me in time; and so the spy would now have me in custody. Therefore Fleetfoot should not have too much blame."

"Ay," grumbled Humphrey. "Thou art ready with thy excuses for thy dog."

"He is all I have, Humphrey," returned Hugo, quietly. "But I promise thee he shall be put in leash on the morrow if he cometh." And he listened anxiously for some sound of his dog's approach. But he heard none.

And now Humphrey's good-nature was quite restored, so that he said: "Think no more of the hound to-night. He hath begun on a partridge. May he not end on a deer; and, if he doth, may the keeper set its loss down to these prowling robber bands. It is well with us thus far."

By this time the horses were fed and supper was over, all having been accomplished in darkness, and Humphrey lay down to sleep.

CHAPTER VI

The part of Yorkshire which they had been traversing abounded in rivers. The Wharfe and the Aire, the first of which joins the Ouse eight miles south, and the second eighteen miles southeast of York, they had already crossed. They were now near the Went, and here, as Hugo discovered the next morning, it was Humphrey's decision to stay a day or two.

"I go no further without a dream," he declared. "Last night I slept too sound to have one. And moreover I wish not to fall in with these galloping king's men. Let them ride up and down till they think us securely hid away in some religious house, since they find us not in the wood. So shall we go the safer on our way to Doncaster."

Hugo had thought much the evening before, and he had resolved to dispute Humphrey in future no more than was necessary. For he now saw that, though he was but a serving-man, Humphrey knew more of Yorkshire woods than his master. He therefore made no objection when Humphrey announced his decision, much to the serving-man's surprise, for he had expected opposition. Finding none, he enlarged his air of importance, and bade Hugo stay where he was while he took the horses down to the stream for water.

Hugo, putting a strong restraint on himself, obeyed, and was rewarded on the serving-man's return with the promise that, as soon as the dog came in and was tied, he might venture forth with Humphrey to explore the region.

"Thou must know," remarked Humphrey, "that we be on the high bank. On the other side of the valley sloping coppices abound, and therein can I show thee many badger holes. Hast ever seen a badger hunt?"

"Nay," answered Hugo.

"I was but twenty years old," continued Humphrey, "when first I came through these woods, and on the bank across the valley from this point I did see a badger hunt. Three men and two dogs did I see, and they five did at length dig out one badger. The old badger was inside the hole taking his sleep, for it was ten o'clock in the morning. And a badger not only sleepeth all day in summer, but day and night in winter. Thou knowest that?"

"Yea," replied Hugo. And added that at his uncle's priory he had occasionally eaten badger meat, which was very good.

"Cured like ham, was it?" inquired Humphrey.

"Yea," responded Hugo.

Humphrey nodded his head approvingly. "A priest," he said, "for knowing and having good eating."

The two sat silent a few moments waiting for Fleetfoot, who did not come, and then Humphrey continued: "The badger hath a thick skin. He goeth into a wasp's nest or a bees' nest, and the whole swarm may sting him and he feeleth it not."

"What doth the badger in wasps' nests and bees' nests?" inquired Hugo.

"Why, he will eat up their grubs. The eggs make footless grubs, and these the badger eateth. My grandsire went a journey through this wood once on a moonlight night. He rode slowly along, and at a certain place was a bees' nest beside the path, and there, full in the moonlight, was a badger rooting out the nest. Out swarmed the bees, and several did sting the horse of my grandsire at the moment when he had taken good aim at the badger with his stick. The horse bolted, and my grandsire found himself lying in the path with his neck all but broken, and the bees taking vengeance on him for the trespass of the badger. He hath had no liking to bees or badgers since that day."

"He still liveth, then?" asked Hugo.

"Ay," returned Humphrey, much pleased at the question. "Hale and hearty he is, and ninety-six years of age."

By common consent both now paused to listen for Fleetfoot. Hearing nothing Humphrey continued, "Didst ever see a tame badger?"

"Nay," was the reply.

"A badger becometh as tame as a dog, if he be taken young. Report hath it that there is great sport in London at the public houses baiting the badger. I know not how it may be."

And now Fleetfoot came. Not joyfully, but slinking, for he knew he had been doing wrong. Three partridges, a fox, and a badger he had slain since Humphrey had seen him, and he wore a guilty look.

"Thou wilt do no more than tie him with the willow thong," observed Humphrey, eyeing Fleetfoot with disfavor. "Were he mine, I should beat him. The king maketh nothing of lopping off a man's hand or foot for such a trespass, or even putting out of his eyes. And should the keepers discover what he hath done, it were all the same as if we had done it."

"Nay, Humphrey," said Hugo, smoothing the dog's head. "Perchance he hath taken no more than the partridge thou sawest."

For answer Humphrey struck lightly the dog's rounded-out side. "Tell me not," he said, "that one partridge hath such a filling power. Else would I feed only on partridges. Moreover, he is a knowing dog, and see how he slinketh. He would not be that cast down for one partridge, I warrant thee."

"It may be thou art right," replied Hugo, as he tied up Fleetfoot.

"Yea, that I may be," returned Humphrey, importantly. "A man that hath dreams of going up a ladder and climbing a tree in the same night is most likely to be right when it cometh to measuring up the trespasses of a straying deerhound. For why should a man be advanced to preferment and honor except that he hath merit? And to dream of going up a ladder and climbing a tree is sure warrant that he hath it. And now fare we forth to see this Brockadale."

Hugo having finished tying Fleetfoot securely with a tether so short that he could not gnaw through it, followed Humphrey, and the dog attempted to follow Hugo, much to Humphrey's satisfaction. "Ay, thou wouldst follow, wouldst thou?" he said. "Bide where thou art with the horses, and think on thy evil deeds." Then turning to the boy he added, "If thou wilt not beat him, Hugo, my chiding may do him some good."

It was a most beautiful little valley that the boy saw when he stood on the edge of a hill on its northern side and gazed down into it, while Humphrey stood by pointing out its features with the air of a proprietor. Green and lovely it stretched away to the southeast some two miles, as Humphrey told him. Through it flowed the Went, bending and turning, its banks lined with osiers and willows. Wooded hills were the northern, and sloping coppices the southern boundary of the vale.

The two had not ventured out into the open. They were still in the shelter of the trees. "The Normans rule, and honest men must skulk and hide," observed Humphrey, with some bitterness.

"Lord De Aldithely is a Norman," remarked Hugo. "So also am I."

"Ay," rejoined Humphrey, "but all Normans are not alike bad. Thou art not the king, moreover, nor is my lord, who is an honest man and standeth bravely by the people, and is opposed to murder and robbery. Therefore is he fled, and therefore is our young lord

Josceline in danger, and therefore are we skulking and hiding and leading the king's men this chase. The times be evil; and who knoweth what shall amend them?"

Hugo did not reply. His eye had caught sight of the flash of sunlight on steel down the valley, and he pointed it out to Humphrey.

"Up! up!" cried Humphrey. "Up into yon spreading oak at the edge of the vale. There shall we be concealed, and yet see all."

"They come from toward Doncaster, do they not?" asked Hugo when they were safely out of sight among the branches.

"Ay," answered Humphrey. "Nor was it for naught that I did sleep too sound to dream last night, else might we have been on the way to Doncaster, and so, perchance, have met them."

The party drew nearer, and soon the keen eyes of Humphrey and Hugo resolved them into three men-at-arms led by Walter Skinner.

"Three soldiers and a king's man to take a boy and a man!" laughed Humphrey. "It must be that they have a good opinion of our bravery."

"Or of thy cunning," said Hugo, to whom Humphrey had a short while before revealed all that had befallen him in Ferrybridge.

"Oh, ay," answered Humphrey, complacently. "I have my share, no doubt. A man doth not live forty years with treachery on all sides of him and learn nothing.

My head had been off my shoulders ere this, had not some measure of cunning done its part to keep it on. They will beat up the whole forest hereabout for us, I doubt not. If I get a good dream to-night, we go on to-morrow."

Hugo smiled. He thought it strange that a man so sensible, in many respects, as Humphrey should pin such faith to dreams. So he said teasingly: "How if thou get not the dream to-night, nor yet to-morrow night? Do we bide here until the dream come, if that be next Michaelmas?"

The serving-man seemed puzzled. Then he answered: "Nay, to be sure. Then would the summer be done; and, moreover, I never went so long without the right dream in my life."

Nearer and nearer drew the horsemen until, in the vale just opposite and below Hugo and Humphrey, they dismounted. "Here do we stop," said Walter Skinner. "I warrant you they be hereabouts, else have the fat priests lied when they denied they were in abbey and priory."

"Ay," answered one of the men-at-arms. "They be hereabouts, no doubt, if they be not farther to the east, when thy fellow will catch them if we miss them. I marvel thou hast not come up with them before now. Thou sayest this is the third day of their flight?"

This seeming to reflect on the ability of the pompous little Walter Skinner, he frowned. And drawing himself up importantly he said, "The young lord hath to his servant a Saxon who knoweth well these parts."

"Some deer-stealer, without doubt," observed the man-at-arms.

"And he goeth not straight forward," continued Walter Skinner, "else had I met him. But he creepeth here, and hideth there, and goeth in retired paths."

"And all to balk thee!" said the big man-at-arms, regarding with scarce concealed contempt the little strutting spy.

There was that in the manner of the man-at-arms that nettled Walter Skinner, so that he became more pompous than before and, resolved to show the soldier how high he stood in the king's counsel, he said haughtily: "Why, it were best he balk me, if he knew what will come to his young master when I find him. King John, as thou knowest, hath a special hatred toward his father, Lord De Aldithely."

"De Aldithely, sayest thou?" interrupted the man-at-arms.

"Ay, and he is resolved the son shall not live, no more than his own nephew Arthur."

"And he will put him to death?" asked the man-at-arms.

"Why, not speedily," answered Walter Skinner, importantly, "but cat and mouse fashion, by which he will be the longer dying, and his father the more tormented. He will speedily give orders also to raze his castle as a nest of traitors."

"Whence hadst thou this?" demanded the man-at-arms.

Walter Skinner stood off and looked at him. Then, with an air of great mystery, he said: "It is whispered about. I may not say more. It becometh me not."

The man-at-arms now rose from the ground where he had thrown himself and mounted his horse. "I seek not the young lord," he said. "I betray no mouse to the cat, least of all the son of the brave De Aldithely. I will back to my own master from whom thou didst borrow me. I will say thou needest me not and hast bid me return. When thou art tired of thy life, say thou otherwise." And he looked meaningly at him.

"I go with thee," said the second man-at-arms, springing from the ground.

"And I also!" exclaimed the third.

In vain Walter Skinner tried to restrain them. They clattered off down the valley whence they had come, and were soon out of sight on their way to Doncaster.

The sound carried well here; the voices of the men were loud; and Hugo and Humphrey, whose ears were keen, heard with consternation all that passed. "I fear it meaneth death to thee also if thou be caught," said Humphrey. "For it is a serious thing to dupe a man of the king's rage. This calleth for dreams, and that right speedily, if we are not to fall into his hands."

The disappointed Walter Skinner made no attempt to depart. "Here will I stay a while," he said, "and berate the folly that did tell them the purpose of the king and the name of the young lord. I did think to raise myself in authority over them by showing that I did know the king's counsel, and, in so doing, I did forget that for

Gulielma Zollinger

murdering of Arthur all men hate him, and few will help him to his will upon others." Moodily he threw himself upon the grass, having staked his horse, and soon left off berating himself by falling into a sound sleep. The sun reached the meridian, and he still slept. It came to be mid-afternoon and still he moved not, for he had ridden hard and had been deprived of his rest the night before. His tethered horse at last whinnied softly and then loudly. And, to the dismay of Hugo and Humphrey, he was answered by their own horses in the thicket. But still the king's man moved not.

"Would that I knew certainly that he sleepeth," said Humphrey, anxiously. "For then we might come down and escape."

"Nay, nay," objected Hugo, earnestly. "Seest thou not how a little sound goeth far here? The rustling of the leaves and rattling of the boughs as we descend might awake him."

Humphrey looked at him. "Ay, poor mouse!" he said. "Mayhap thou art right."

And now Walter Skinner stirred in his slumber. Once more his horse whinnied loudly. Once more the horses in the thicket answered; and the spy, broad awake, sprang to his feet. "Aha, Fortune!" he cried, "thou art with me."

"Nevertheless," observed Humphrey, softly, "if thou hast not dreamed of going up a ladder and climbing a tree, all may not go so well with thee as thou thinkest."

Leaving his horse, the spy climbed the wooded hill, at the top of which he paused just under the oak in which

Hugo and Humphrey were concealed. The horses whinnied no more, though he waited a few moments hoping to hear them. "I will on," he cried impatiently. "'Twas from this direction the answer came." And away he hurried on foot, for he imagined that those he sought were hidden near at hand, and waiting for the night to come ere they resumed their journey. He knew that he alone could not capture them, but if he could get on their trail and dog them unseen till he could get help he would be sure of them.

As soon as the spy was out of sight Humphrey began to descend the tree.

"Whither goest thou?" asked Hugo.

"Thou shalt see," returned Humphrey.

With speed he ran down the hill, breaking a switch of birch as he ran. He hastened to Walter Skinner's horse, cut him loose from his tether, and struck him sharply with the birch rod. Away galloped the horse down the valley, while Humphrey hastened back to his place in the tree. "Fortune may be with him," he said to Hugo, "but his horse is not. Mayhap I need not another dream, for, by the one I had, I think we have got the better of him. Moreover, there will be no more whinnying for our horses to answer."

CHAPTER VII

Till the set of sun and the dusk of the evening the spy pursued the search, now stumbling over a tree root, now catching his foot in a straggling vine, and every now and then sorely struck in the face by the underbrush through which he pushed his way. But, although he was once very near the concealed horses and hound, he found nothing to reward him. The return to the little vale was even more tiresome than the journey from it had been. No moon would shine for an hour, and it was quite dark when he once more reached the oak in which Hugo and Humphrey had stayed all day, but from which they had a few moments before descended.

In climbing the tree, after setting Walter Skinner's horse loose, Humphrey had noticed a hollow in one of the lower branches. "Perchance," he said, "a hedgehog may lodge therein. Knowest thou the ways of hedgehogs?"

"Nay," returned Hugo, indifferently.

"The lad hath lost heart," said Humphrey to himself, "and all because of the words of this little snipe of a king's man and the slowness of the journey. I will not seem to see it." Then he continued as if Hugo had displayed the greatest interest: "I will tell thee, then, that hedgehogs have many ways. I warrant thee this king's man knoweth naught of them, any more than he knoweth the wood. Had he been some men, we had been caught ere now. I fear him not overmuch. For do but see how he is puffed up with undue pride and importance. And let me tell thee that undue pride and importance and good sense dwell not in the same skull. We shall therefore have the better of him."

Hugo made no reply, and Humphrey continued cheerfully: "A hedgehog will find a hollow in a tree, and there he will bide, sleeping all day. At night he will come forth. But first he must reach the ground. And this he will do by rolling into a ball and dropping on the ends of his spines. If the ground is beneath him, no harm is done. If this king's man should be beneath him, I think not that he would cry out that Fortune was with him when the spines of the hedgehog stuck into him."

"And how would the king's man be beneath him?" asked Hugo, dully.

"If the hedgehog be in the hollow of that low branch," answered Humphrey, "and if the king's man should stand under at such time as the hedgehog was ready to drop, then he would be beneath him."

"Yea," observed Hugo. "Many things might come to pass, if thou couldst make all the plans."

Humphrey did not hear the sarcasm in Hugo's tones. He heard only what he was pleased to take as a compliment to his own abilities. "Why, I believe thou art right," he answered. "Were I to make the plans, some that are now at the top would be at the bottom. Thou hast well said. But come. It grows dark. Let us go down ere the king's man come back on his way to the vale."

Slowly they made their way down. "This perching on trees all day is fit to make an old man of a boy," said Humphrey, as he stepped clumsily about on his half-numbed feet.

"Sh!" said Hugo.

Humphrey instantly stood still in the darkness and listened. Weary and slow steps were approaching. They came nearer, and directly under the oak they ceased, for the spy, his pompous manner quite gone, had stopped to rest a little. And now a rustling in the branches above was heard. Eagerly the spy looked up and strained his eyes to see. "Josceline! son of Lord De Aldithely!" he called, "I arrest thee in the king's name. Thou darest not oppose me. Yield thyself, and come down!"

And just then the hedgehog which Humphrey had surmised might be in the hollow, moved a little farther along on the branch, rustling the leaves as he did so. In the darkness the face of the spy was still turned upward. He had forgotten that he was alone and unaided. And he thought only of getting hold of the boy he sought.

"Come down!" he repeated. "Come down, I say! Make no dallying!"

And then the hedgehog rolled himself into a ball and came down plump into the face of Walter Skinner.

"Ugh! what have we here?" sputtered the spy, starting back.

Hugo and Humphrey did not wait for him to discover, but stepping softly away they went to the thicket, where the hungry animals gave them a warm welcome, and where they thoroughly enjoyed the first meal they had had since morning. Their supper eaten, Humphrey untied horses and hound, to lead them to water.

"Thou wilt be caught," objected Hugo, nervously.

"Not I," returned Humphrey, easily. "I fear not the spy to-night. If he heareth aught, he will think another hedgehog about to drop upon him. Come thou with me and see."

Hugo obediently rose from the couch of boughs where he had thrown himself, and took the thong of willow from Humphrey's hand to lead Fleetfoot. The serving-man was right. So far as Walter Skinner was concerned they had no more to fear that night. His face was lacerated; and by the time Hugo and Humphrey started from the thicket he had discovered the loss of his horse. It had been better for him if his drinking-horn, from which he now took copious draughts, had been lost also.

"The kind of fortune that is with him, I should not wish to be with me," observed Humphrey, when they had returned safely to the thicket. "I will now to sleep and see what sort of a dream cometh."

Much cheered in spirit, Hugo also lay down to sleep. His courage came back, and he felt that let the journey take as long as it would he was equal to it.

The moon had now risen, and by its light Richard Wood, the other spy, and his borrowed men-at-arms came riding through one of the glades of the forest southward to the vale. Richard Wood had not the overweening vanity of Walter Skinner; he had not taken his borrowed men-at-arms into his confidence concerning the king's plans in order to make it appear that he stood high in counsel; neither had he revealed the name of the lad they sought. The men-at-arms had, therefore, all three remained with him, and were as eager as he on the chase. They were pushing on now to the vale to camp for the night, because they could find there both grass and water. And, in the same spot where Walter Skinner had slept before, they came upon a figure reclining in full sight in the moonlight.

"There lieth one of them," said a man-at-arms, "but I see not the other."

"Thou mayest be sure the other is not far off," observed the second.

"Thou shalt see how quickly I will awake him out of sleep," cried the third, as he spurred his horse toward him and pricked him sharply with the point of his lance.

"Ugh!" grunted the half-drunken Walter Skinner. "But I have had enough of hedgehogs for one night." And he sat up sleepily.

"And is it thou, Walter Skinner?" exclaimed Richard Wood.

"Why, who should it be?" answered Walter Skinner, peevishly.

"Thou art a brave pursuer!" said Richard Wood.

"Where be thy men-at-arms? and where is thy horse?"

"My men-at-arms are returned to their master," replied Walter Skinner, while those of Richard Wood drew near to learn the whereabouts of their companions. "As for my horse, I wot not what is become of him."

"And wherefore did thy men-at-arms play thee false?" demanded Richard Wood.

"Softly!" replied Walter Skinner, his small, cracked voice more cracked than usual. "Ask me not so many questions if thou wouldst not see me dead before thee."

Richard Wood regarded him sternly. "Thou must be moonstruck," he said at length. "When ever heard any one of a man dying of the questions asked of him?"

"Thou mistakest my meaning," returned Walter Skinner, a trace of his pomposity returning. "Thou askest me questions. If I answer thee false, I lie. If I answer thee true, I die. And truly, death were not much worse than this lacerated face of mine."

"Why, how now!" demanded Richard Wood. "How camest thy face lacerated?"

"One Master Hedgehog of this forest hath paid me his attentions too closely."

For a moment Richard Wood was silent. Then he said: "Answer me truly. It behooveth me to know the truth in this matter. Why did thy men-at-arms leave thee?"

"I did but let fall the king's purpose toward the young lord, and name his father, De Aldithely, and they fell off from me as I had been myself a murderer. Bade me uphold their lying speech that I had no need of their services on pain of death, and so left me."

And now one of the men-at-arms spoke. "We be not knaves," he said. "We had not thought to lead the youth to death, but to honorable captivity for a brief while. Nor did we know the lad ye seek was son to De Aldithely. Wherefore we also leave ye, and if ye say why, your lives shall answer for it. We have no mind to be marks for the king's vengeance. He that would crush the Archdeacon of Norwich with a cope of lead will have no mercy on a man-at-arms that thwarted him. Wherefore, say why we left ye, if ye think best." And, riding a little way off, all three encamped by themselves for the night.

"It seemeth that the best way to earn hatred and contempt is to serve this King John," remarked Richard Wood, thoughtfully.

"Ay, and the attention of hedgehogs also," returned Walter Skinner, thickly. "And the loss of horse and food, and the loss of the quarry also, if we strike not the trail again. And though we have not the service of the men-at-arms, be sure we shall pay for it as if we had it to their master. I would I had a troop of mercenaries to rent out. It were easier than such scouring of the country as this. Moreover we do exceed our office. The king said not to me, 'Walter Skinner, scour the country.' Nay, the king said naught to me on the matter. 'Twas his favorite, Sir Thomas De Lany, that bade me watch the castle from the tree; and there might I be now in comfort, if this hare-brained youth had not run away. He should have stayed at the castle till the coming of Robert Sadler and the troop.

My face had not been thus lacerated had the youth known his duty and done it."

"Why, how makest thou all this?" demanded Richard Wood, contemptuously. "The king careth not whose hand delivereth the youth, so that he be delivered. That we have not already caught him is the fault of thyself alone. Hadst thou but held thy tongue, we had had with us to-night six men-at-arms, and had, erelong, run down the game. In the morning I go to Hubert le Falconer and hire from him six more - three for thee, and three for me. Then do thou be silent as to the king's purpose, and this mischief of thy making may be repaired. Thou mayest look as if thou wert bursting with wisdom, if it please thee, but see that thou give no enlightening word to thy followers."

"Ay, thou mayest lay the burden of all mishaps on me," returned Walter Skinner, pettishly. "But I promise not that I will speak no word, if it seemeth to me best to speak. It is not every one in the king's employ. Not every one is out scouring the country for a lord's son. And if one may not speak of his honors, why hath he them?"

"Honors!" exclaimed Richard Wood, with contempt. "There be few would call such work as thine an honor. To skulk, to spy, to trap another to his destruction, why, that is what most call knaves' work, and he who doth it is despised. Yea, even though he do it for a king."

"Thy loss doth set but sourly on thy stomach, Richard Wood," said Walter Skinner, stubbornly. "It is an honor to serve the king. Ay, even though he be a bad one like this. And, I say, if one is not to speak of honors, why hath he them?"

"For other people to see, varlet. What others *see* of thy *honors*, as thou callest them, they can mayhap endure. But when thou pratest of thy honors, thou dost but enrage them. Wilt thou give me thy word to be silent?"

"Nay, that will I not," retorted Walter Skinner. "I be as good a man as thou, and not a bear in leading. When I will to speak, I speak; whether it be of the king's matters or my own."

"Thou hast said," returned Richard Wood, rising. "In the morning I hire three men-at-arms from Hubert le Falconer for myself. Pursue thou the chase as seemeth thee best. We hunt no more in company."

With the first morning light the men-at-arms mounted their horses and rode toward Doncaster, Richard Wood rode north to seek his needed men-at-arms from Hubert le Falconer, and only Walter Skinner was left horseless and breakfastless in the vale. He had no mind to remain there in that condition, and so betook himself to the nearest priory, confident that, in the king's name, he could there procure both food and a horse, and perhaps a leech to ease his wounded face.

Hugo and Humphrey were also early astir, the serving-man performing his morning tasks with such a particularly cheerful air that Hugo smiled and inquired, "Hadst thou a dream last night?"

"Ay," answered Humphrey, in triumph. "I say not with that little spy, 'Aha, Fortune! thou art with me,' and then go out to meet a hedgehog. But this I say, that I did dream of bees and of following them, which betokeneth gain or profit. And therefore go we not toward Doncaster."

"Why not toward Doncaster down this Brockadale?" asked Hugo.

"The vale is well enough," replied Humphrey, "but it extendeth only two miles after all. We must make haste to-day. I do remember that two spies did pursue us at the beginning. It may be that the other hath neither lost his horse nor met a hedgehog to discourage him. And, moreover, what is to hinder him from having three men-at-arms to his help like his fellow? Nay, Hugo, we go not through the vale, but make we what haste we may through short cuts and little used paths."

"And whither do we go?" asked Hugo.

"I will tell thee that we seek the marshy Isle of Axholme to the east of the river Don. There will be room therein for us to hide away, and there no king's men will look for us moreover."

"Why?" asked Hugo.

"Why, lad?" repeated Humphrey. "Why, because they will not. Will a king's man trust himself in such a boggy place? Nay. Moreover, I fell in with this one that hath so lately followed us at Ferrybridge, which is a sure sign that we should meet the other at Doncaster."

"But - " began Hugo.

"I tell thee," interrupted Humphrey, "I did dream of

bees and of following them. We go straight to this Isle of Axholme. Vex me no more."

Hugo opened his mouth to remonstrate still further, but, happening to remember his determination not to oppose Humphrey except through necessity, he closed it again. Seeing which, Humphrey regarded him approvingly, and even went to the length of expressing his approbation in words.

"Thou art learning to keep thyself under," he said. "Thou hast but just opened thy mouth to speak and shut it again with thy words unsaid. When one hath no knack at dreams to help him on, the best thing for him is the power to shut his mouth. An open mouth maketh naught but trouble. Thou didst wish to see more of the vale, and so thou shalt. Thou shalt see so much of it as thou canst while the horses and hound drink their fill before starting."

CHAPTER VIII

The Isle of Axholme, to which Humphrey was determined to go, was a marshy tract of ground in the northwest part of what is now Lincolnshire, and its eastern boundary was the Trent River. It was some eighteen miles long from north to south, and some five miles wide from east to west. On its north side was the wide mouth of the Ouse; the river Idle was south of it, and west of it was the Don. In the time of the Romans there had been a forest here which they had cut down, and the low, level land afterward became a marsh. At this time few trees were to be found there. But there were thickets of underbrush and patches of rank grass, as well as pools and boggy places; and Humphrey was right in thinking the place comparatively safe from pursuit. Especially so as the pursuers would naturally think that the young lord Josceline would push on as rapidly as possible, that he might get across to France to join his father.

"I go no more where the crowd goeth," declared Humphrey, when they were on their way. "How many, thinkest thou, of all that be abroad in these parts pass through Doncaster? Why, near all. We need not to show ourselves further to draw pursuit. This is now the fourth day since we set out, and my lady and Josceline must be well along in their journey. I would I knew the doings of William Lorimer at the castle. He is a brave

Gulielma Zollinger

man and a true, though he would never tell me his plans that he might take my counsel. He ever made naught of dreams and spake lightly of omens. I hope he may not fare the worse for it."

Hugo made no reply. He, too, was wondering about how things were going at the castle, but he kept his thoughts to himself.

"Now I will tell thee," said Humphrey, pausing and turning in his saddle, "when thou seest me draw rein and hold up my hand, do thou stop instantly. There be many robbers in this wood, and we have them to fear as well as king's men. And hold Fleetfoot fast. Let him not escape thee."

Hugo promised to obey in these particulars, and Humphrey, for a short distance, put his horse to the trot with Hugo following close behind him. All that day they turned and wound through the forest, going fast where they dared, and at other times creeping silently along. To Hugo it seemed they must be lost; but, when darkness fell, they had reached the edge of the Isle of Axholme, and, putting the horses through the Don, were safe in its marshy wastes.

"Here be no keepers and rangers," said Humphrey, exultingly. "And here may we kill and eat what we choose, while Fleetfoot may hunt for himself. We stir not till the moon rise, and then we seek a place to sleep," he concluded, patting the wet coat of the horse he rode.

Hugo said nothing. He did not know it, but he was nervous. All day he had been on the alert, and now to stay perfectly still in this strange, silent place, not daring to stir in the darkness lest he splash into some pool, or mire in a bog; with his eyes attempting to see, when it was too dark to see anything but the glow-worms in the grass and the will-o'-the-wisp, was an added strain.

Two hours went by, and the curtain of darkness began to lift. The moonlight made visible a fringe of small trees and the shine of the water on whose bank they grew. The breeze rose and sighed and whistled through rush and reed. An owl hooted, and then Humphrey, who had been nodding on his horse's back, suddenly became very wide awake.

"Hast been here before, Hugo?" he cried cheerily.

"Nay," answered the boy, listlessly.

"No more have I," returned Humphrey. "But what of that? A man who hath proper dreams may be at home in all places. I will now seek out our resting-place, and do thou and Fleetfoot follow me." So saying, he chirruped to his patient horse and led the way carefully; for, however much Humphrey imagined he depended on dreams, he generally exercised as good judgment and care as he was able. To-night weary Hugo had forgotten that Humphrey was his servant, and, as such, bound to obey him. He felt himself nothing but a tired and homesick boy, and was glad himself to obey the faithful Saxon, while he thought regretfully of his uncle the prior, Lady De Aldithely, Josceline, and the valiant William Lorimer.

It was not Humphrey's intention to go farther that night than absolutely necessary; and a little later he dismounted and stamped his feet with satisfaction.

Gulielma Zollinger

"Here be solid ground enough and to spare for us and the horses and hound," he said, "and here will we rest."

A lone, scrubby tree was at hand, and to that Humphrey made fast the horses and dog. "No fire to-night. Thy cloak must be thy protection from the damp," he said. "But the swamp is not so damp as the king's dungeon, nor so dismal. So let us eat and sleep."

Hugo said nothing. He ate a morsel with a swelling heart, and then, in silence, lay down. He was beginning to find leading evil men a merry chase a rather unpleasant business.

In the moonlight Humphrey looked at him. "He is a good lad," he thought, "and seemeth no more to me like a stranger. I begin to see that he seemed no stranger to my lady neither. My lord will make him his page, no doubt, if he getteth safely over to France. France is a good country when a bad king ruleth at home." Then faithful Humphrey, the animals fed, himself lay down to sleep.

It was late the next morning when Hugo awoke. Humphrey had been stirring two hours; and the first thing the boy's eyes rested upon was a little fire made of bits of punky wood collected by Humphrey; and spitted above the coals were two small birds roasting.

"Ay, lad!" cried Humphrey. "Open thine eyes now, and we will to breakfast presently. What sayest thou to a peewit each? Is that not better than brawn?"

Hugo smiled and arose at once. His despondency of

the night before was gone, together with his fatigue, and he looked about him with interest. To the left were reeds some twelve feet tall which fringed a pool; to the right, thick sedge that fringed another; and they seemed to be on a sort of tiny, grassy isle, though the water which divided them from the next bit of solid earth could, in some places, be stepped across. The sun shone with agreeable warmth. There were frequent whirrs of wings in the air as small flocks of game birds rose from the water and sedge near by.

"This is not the wood nor is it Brockadale; but here one may breathe a little without having his eyes looking on all sides for an enemy," said Humphrey, with satisfaction. "It is the turn of the peewits to look out. Knowest thou the peewit?"

"On the table only," answered Hugo, pleasantly.

"Ay," observed Humphrey. "Thine uncle, the prior, hath many a fat feast in the priory, I warrant thee. But here thou shalt see the peewit at home. Had we but come in April, we had had some eggs as well as birds to eat."

Humphrey had made a fresh meal cake in the embers, and the two - boy and serving-man - now sat devouring birds and cake with great appetites.

"Thou knowest the pigeon?" asked Humphrey.

"Yea," replied Hugo.

"The peewit is the size of a pigeon."

"So I should guess," remarked Hugo.

"There be those that call it the lapwing," pursued Humphrey.

"My uncle, the prior, is of the number," smiled Hugo.

"Ay, priests ever have abundance of names for everything. It cometh, no doubt, from knowing Latin and other outlandish gibberish."

Hugo smiled indulgently. His feeling toward Humphrey had, during the last day, undergone a complete change. And, though he was but a Saxon serving-man, the heart of the boy had now an affection for him. Humphrey was quick to detect it, and he too smiled.

"Had the peewit short legs like the pigeon," he continued, "and did he but want what they call the crest on the back of his head, and could you see only the back of the bird, he might be thought a pigeon, since he shineth on the back like a peacock in all colors blue and green can make when mixed together. But when he standeth on his somewhat long legs, and thou seest that his under parts be white, why, even a Frenchman would know he was no pigeon, but must be the peewit or lapwing. And I warrant thee we shall eat our fill of peewits if we remain here long."

"When thinkest thou of going?" asked Hugo, interestedly.

"Why, that I know not. I would fain have another dream. I know not how it may be with other men, but when I am right weary I dream not. Which I take as an omen not to stir till I be rested and ready to use my wits. Thou hast noticed that weariness dulleth the wits?"

"Yea," replied Hugo.

"Why, I have seen in my time many fall into grievous snares from nothing more than being weary, and so, dull of sight and hearing. But here cometh Fleetfoot sleek and satisfied. I did but turn him loose two hours ago, and I warrant thee he hath had a fine meal. I will make him fast once more, and then we go farther into the island to seek another resting-place for the night. This is too near the edge of the marsh, and too near the Don."

Mounting the horses, and with Fleetfoot once more in leash, they set out, Humphrey picking his way and Hugo following. And by mid-day they had come to what Humphrey decided was probably the best location for them on the island. It was another solid, grassy place, and was graced with three little scrub trees which gave them a leafy roof under which to lie. From the fringe of neighboring rushes the two cut enough to strew their resting-place thickly, and so protect their bodies from the damp ground. Then Humphrey dug a shallow fire-pit at the north, and, after their mid-day meal, set diligently about collecting a store of fuel. Little was to be found solid enough to cook with, and that little he stored carefully apart, reserving a great heap of dead rushes and reeds for the blaze which was to ward off the night dampness and make them comfortable. In all these labors Hugo bore his share, for the two, by tacit consent, were no longer master and man but comrades in need and danger.

In collecting the reeds they took few from their immediate neighborhood, wishing to be as protected

Gulielma Zollinger

from chance observation as possible. And they found their wanderings in search of fuel full of interest. At some distance from their camping-place they came upon a muddy shallow. And there on the bank Hugo saw his first avoset or "scooper," as Humphrey called him. The bird was resting from his labors when the two first observed him. Though the ooze was soft the bird did not sink into it. There he stood, his wide-webbed toes supporting him on the surface of the ooze, and it seemed a long way from his feet up his blue legs to his black-and-white body. But the oddest thing about him was his long, curved, and elastic bill turning up at the end. The bird had not observed them, and presently set to work scooping through the mud after worms. Then he waded out a little way into the shallow, where he did not stay long, for, catching sight of Hugo and Humphrey, he rose a little in the air and flew swiftly away. Farther on they came upon a wading crane with an unlucky snake in his mouth. And still farther away they caught sight of a mother duck swimming with her young brood upon a pool. And every now and then a frog plumped into the water. But nowhere did they discover, by sight or sound, another human being beside themselves.

When darkness fell the glow-worms shone once more, the will-o'-the-wisp danced, and the owls hooted. The fire of dead rushes and reeds, fed by the patient Humphrey, blazed brightly and shed a grateful warmth upon their sheltered resting-place under the three scrub trees. And, lying at ease upon the rushes, the hours of darkness went by till, when the moon arose, the fire had died down, Hugo slept, and Humphrey had gone in search of a favoring dream.

Near Doncaster that night camped Richard Wood with

his three newly hired men-at-arms; while within the town at an inn called the Green Dragon lay Walter Skinner. He was newly equipped with a horse. "I need no men-at-arms," he said to himself, "nor will I hire them. I will catch the young lord and his serving-man with arrow and bow if I but come up with them again."

And that night, safe out of the forest of Galtus, Lady De Aldithely and her party encamped on the border of Scotland.

That night also Robert Sadler, pausing to rest on his return journey to the castle, looked often at the package he carried, and wondered what it contained.

That night also the valiant William Lorimer and his men-at-arms rested from their labors well satisfied. For, while the moat at the great gate held only its usual allowance of water, by means of the new dam they had constructed, that part of the moat near the postern was level full.

The next morning marked the beginning of the sixth day of their journey, and Humphrey rose with unimpaired cheerfulness. Once more Hugo's waking eyes beheld two peewits spitted over the coals and a meal cake baking in the embers. "I did dream of gold last night," said Humphrey, by way of a morning greeting. "Knowest thou what that betokeneth?"

"Nay," responded Hugo, pleasantly.

"It betokeneth success in thy present undertaking after first meeting with difficulties. We have met with difficulties, and what were they but the king's men? They be now behind us, and success is to be ours. But come thou to breakfast now. To-morrow morn we set forth again."

CHAPTER IX

On this, their last day in the Isle of Axholme, Hugo and Humphrey took up the occupation of the day before, but with more deliberation. And they went in a different direction, - southeast, toward the Trent.

"It is this way we journey on the morrow with the horses," remarked Humphrey. "It is as well to see what the way is like while we gather our store of reeds and rushes. For I did dream of gold, which betokeneth success in our present undertaking, and success ever resteth on good care and good judgment. And so let us see where the solid places be and where the bogs lie. And do thou note well the course so that we may run it with safety and speed if need be. And we will not gather the reeds and rushes till we return."

"Meanest thou to walk to the Trent, then, to-day, and back again?" questioned Hugo. And by this time he had so far forgotten the difference in their stations that there was respect in his tone, which Humphrey was quick to notice.

"Yea, lad," answered the serving-man, kindly. "It is only a few miles. It is not well to risk miring the horses when I did dream of gold last night."

Hugo smiled. He was beginning to see that, while the

superstition of the age, and particularly of his condition, had, to a certain extent, a hold on Humphrey, his course was really directed by sturdy common-sense; and he wondered no more at Lady De Aldithely's trust in him.

The two were well on their way, and Richard Wood and his men-at-arms were scouring the forest near Doncaster, when Walter Skinner walked out to the stables of the Green Dragon to see to his horse. His face was still painful, and he desired to vent some of his spleen on the unlucky groom, whoever he might be, who had his horse in charge. He found the horse tied to a ring in the stable wall, and the groom having a sorry time of it, since every time the groom touched him with comb or brush the animal backed, or turned, or laid back his ears and snapped with his teeth. For the monks at the priory had furnished the king's man, on his compulsion, with the worst horse in their stables.

"Here be a beast fit for the Evil One and for nobody else," grumbled the sorely tried groom. "I am like to be killed for my pains in trying to smooth his coat for him."

The groom was a tall, overgrown fellow of nineteen, with a vacant face and an ever-running tongue. He now stood stock still upon the approach of Walter Skinner and gazed at him. He would have done the same if any creature possessed of the power of locomotion had come into his view. But of that Walter Skinner was ignorant. To him the gaze of the groom seemed honor and respect toward himself, and even, perhaps, awe. And he was at once mollified.

" My horse is a beast of mettle , " he observed

complacently when the groom had returned to his work.

"Ay, and I would that his master, the Evil One, had the grooming of him," was the retort.

"Why, how now, sirrah! Dost thou slander the horse which is a gift from Mother Church to the king's work? Thou art a knave, and no doubt art but unfit for thy task this morn through over-late carousing last night."

"Thou mayest call it carousing, if thou wilt," said the groom, sulkily. "I did come from Gainsborough yesterday. And in the dark, as I did come, I saw a flaming fire in the Isle of Axholme."

"And what meanest thou to tell me of that?" demanded Walter Skinner, sternly. "Thou wert no doubt so drunk that a will-o'-the-wisp in that boggy place did seem to thee even as a flaming fire. Why dost thou not stand to my horse and get down with him? He hath already backed and turned a matter of some miles."

The groom stopped and looked at him indignantly. "I may be but a groom," he said, "but the Isle of Axholme I know from a child, every bog in it. And I did go to the fire, which was a bit out of my way, but, being my only pleasure on the journey, I did take it. And there on the rushes lay a young lord, and his serving-man did feed the fire with reeds."

"Thou didst see that?" cried Walter Skinner, in great excitement. "Make haste with the beast, sirrah. Here is a coin for thee, good groom. I do now see thou wert never drunken in thy life. Make haste with the horse."

The groom stared at him foolishly. "Why, who could make haste with such a beast?" he said at length.

"Then stay not to finish thy work," cried Walter Skinner, impatiently. "Bring saddle and bridle. I must away instantly. But do thou first describe to me the place where thou didst see the fire."

"The place," said the groom, deliberately, while he examined the coin Walter Skinner had given him. "Thou dost go till thou comest to it. A turn here and a turn there mayhap thou must make, and thou wilt find it a little solid place with three scrub trees upon it. It is a matter of a short distance from the south end of the Isle, and thou wilt not fail to know it when thou seest it."

With this not over-clear direction Walter Skinner was obliged to be content. Bidding the groom to bring the horse to the door of the inn at once, he hurried away, paid his reckoning, examined carefully the string of his bow, and looked over his store of arrows. "And now, Josceline, son of Lord De Aldithely," he said, "my arrow will bid thee halt this time, and not my voice. And thou, Richard Wood, who didst say, 'We hunt no more in company,' what wouldst thou give to know of this place in the Isle of Axholme? And thou mayst have thy men-at-arms to bear thee company, and to pay for when thou art done with them. They cost thee more than a bow and some arrows cost me, nor will they do thee one half the good."

So thinking he bestrode the vicious beast which backed and plunged about the inn yard, and from which the grooms and the watching maids fled in all directions. Walter Skinner, however, was not to be unseated, and, the horse being headed in the right direction, his next plunge carried him out of the yard and fairly started him on his way, the spur of his rider giving him no permission to halt for a moment.

"And now," thought Walter Skinner, when he had crossed the Don and was free of the town, "what said the knave groom? I must go till I come to it. Ay, and who knoweth when that shall be, and who knoweth the way in this pitfall of bogs? Three scrub trees, saith he, and all together on one little solid place. I would I might see three little scrub trees."

His horse had been over the Isle before and, being given his head, began to pick his way so cleverly that Walter Skinner was still further elated. He sat up pompously and pictured himself a courtier at the palace as a reward for this day's work. "For I lean not to golden rewards alone," he said. "No doubt it can be managed that from this day I begin to rise. The king hath advanced baser men than I, let Richard Wood think as he will in the matter."

And now he descried the three little scrub trees; but he saw not the horses, they having been taken to another islet for pasture; nor Fleetfoot, who had gone with Hugo and Humphrey.

"The knave groom spake true," said Walter Skinner, with satisfaction. "There be the rushes on which they lie, and there the ashes of the fire. I will seek out a convenient hiding-place in the reeds, and to-night, when the fire blazeth bright, then shall my arrows sing."

So saying he sought a place of concealment for himself

and his horse, and, having found it, and tied the horse securely, he lay down well satisfied.

Hugo and Humphrey did not return till toward evening. They had caught some fish in the Trent and roasted them on the coals for their dinner, and afterward had come leisurely back, enjoying the scenes and sights of the marsh.

From his covert Walter Skinner saw them come, each leading a horse which he had stopped to get from the islet pasture, while Fleetfoot lagged behind on a little hunting expedition of his own. The spy drew his bow and sighted. "Yea," he said to himself, "no doubt I can do it. And what is an arrow wound more or less when one would win the favor of the king? The lad or his servant may die of it. But what is death? It is e'en what every man sooner or later must meet. And it is the king's favor I will have, come what may to these runaways." Then he laid down the bow and arrow and took a long drink from his horn. "When the flames shoot high and they be in the strong light of the blaze, then will I shoot," he said. "And it is their own fault if they be hit. They should have remained in the castle where Robert Sadler arriveth this same night."

Hugo and Humphrey had not before been on such thoroughly amicable terms as they were to-night. The boy, so much like his young master, had, unconsciously to Humphrey, won his way into the heart of the serving-man; while Hugo had learned in their few days' companionship to feel toward Humphrey as his faithfulness deserved. So, while the fire blazed up and all remained in darkness outside of its circle, Humphrey entertained Hugo with tales of his early life, to which the boy listened with appreciation. "Ay, lad," said Humphrey, when half an hour had gone by and he paused in his story to look at him with approval, "thou hast the ears of my lady herself, who is ever ready to listen to what I would say."

And then came a whistling arrow, shot by an unsteady, drunken hand, and another, and another, none of which wounded either boy or man, since Hugo was still defended by his shirt of mail, and Humphrey wore a stout gambeson.

Instantly Humphrey started up and, snatching a great bunch of long, flaming reeds to serve him for a light, ran in the direction whence the arrows had come. Hugo, catching up an armful of reeds yet unlighted to serve when those Humphrey carried should burn out, hurried after him. Soon they had found the covert and the spy, and, tossing his torch to Hugo, the serving-man rushed at him.

"And wouldst thou slay my dear lad?" he cried. "Thou snipe!"

"Stand back!" sputtered the spy. "Lay not thy hands upon me. I serve the king."

"Ay, and thou shalt find what it is to serve the king," cried Humphrey, seizing him by the shoulders and dragging him along. "Yon is his horse," he said, turning to Hugo. "Cut him loose."

The boy obeyed and, with a snort, the animal was off.

"Thou shalt be well punished for this deed," threatened the spy. "The steed was the gift of the prior of St. Edmund's."

"Talk not of punishment," cried the enraged Humphrey; "thou who wouldst slay my dear lad. Lead to the right, lad!" he cried. "I do know a miry pool. It will not suck him down, but it will cause him some labor to get out of it."

Hugo, bearing the torch, obeyed, and shortly they had reached the pool which Humphrey had discovered the day before. Grasping his shoulders yet more firmly, and fairly lifting the little spy from his feet, the stalwart Humphrey set him down with a thud in the sticky mud. "There thou mayest stand like a reed or a rush," he said. "I would thou wert as worthy as either."

A moment the spy stood there in water up to his knees while Hugo and Humphrey, by the light of the ever-renewed torch of reeds, watched him. Then he began to try to extricate himself. But when he pulled one foot loose, it was only to set the other more securely in the mud.

"Ay, lad," observed Humphrey, with satisfaction. "He danceth very well, but somewhat slowly. Leave we him to his pleasure while we go seek for his bow and arrows. It were not well that he should shoot at us again."

"Thou villain!" cried the half-drunken Walter Skinner; "when I am a lord in His Majesty's service thou shalt hear of this night's work."

"Ay, Sir Stick-in-the-Mud," responded Humphrey, indifferently. "When that day cometh I am content to hear of it." Then he led the way back to Walter Skinner's hiding-place, while Hugo followed. And there they found the bow, which was of yew with a silken string. And with it was a goodly store of ash arrows tipped with steel and winged with goose feathers.

"We be not thieves, lad," said Humphrey, "else might we add these to our store." So saying, he broke the arrows and flung them away, cut the bow-string in pieces, and flung the bow far from him into the water. "Had these been in a steady hand," he said, "it might now be ill with us. Perchance the spy doth not now cry out, 'Aha, Fortune! thou art with me.' And now let us back to our couch of rushes, there to wait till the moon rise, which will be some three hours. And rest we in darkness. We may not have more fire to make us targets, perchance, for the other spy."

In silence the two lay down on the rushes, Hugo full of excitement and nervously listening for the whistle of another arrow. And, much to the boy's astonishment, in five minutes the faithful Humphrey was sound asleep.

He continued to sleep until the beams of the rising moon struck him full in the face, when he awoke. "Hast slept, lad?" he asked.

"Nay," replied Hugo.

"Thou shouldst have done so. Perchance the time cometh shortly when we dare not sleep; for I did dream of being taken by the constable, which signifieth want of wit, and so I know not what to do. But we may not bide here. On we must go, and make the best of what wit we have." He rose from the rushes and, followed by Hugo, went to the horses and put Fleetfoot once more in leash. Then, each having mounted, he led the way toward the track they had marked out the day before.

"If the spy be not too lazy, he will doubtless be free of the miry pool in the morning," observed Humphrey. "And he might as well have dreamed of being taken by the constable, for if he lacketh not the wit to keep him from a worse case, I know not the measure of a man's mind. And that should I know, having observed not only my lord, but the valiant William Lorimer also."

CHAPTER X

It was the afternoon of this same day in which Walter Skinner had ventured into the wilds of the Isle of Axholme, there to try to catch Hugo and Humphrey. At the same time Robert Sadler was galloping on his way from the town of Chester to the castle, eager to meet the troop, for his journey was now almost accomplished. Sir Thomas De Lany had promised him his reward, - a certain sum of money; he had also promised the troop he had borrowed to help him a reward in addition to the sum he was to pay to their master, even a share of the plunder of the castle. Robert Sadler knew this, and he had quite decided that the package he carried would properly fall to him when her ladyship should be left without a son and without treasure. He therefore had bestowed it carefully out of sight of the king's spies and their borrowed troop, whom he was now expecting to meet. He had said nothing about the presence of Hugo at the castle and his great resemblance to Josceline; for he was of a mind to deliver up Hugo and keep back Josceline, since, by so doing, he might have hope of winning another reward from the king in addition to the one he should receive from Sir Thomas.

"It is a long head that I have," he said to himself with pride. "And these knave spies shall find it not so easy to come to the bottom of my mind. They think I am but

Irish, and so to be despised. And what be they but English? They shall find I will know how to have the better of them."

The sun was within half an hour of setting when he drew rein at the oak which was the scene of their appointed meeting. If he had been eager, the others had been no less so, and at once Sir Thomas and one of his aids advanced to meet him, while, at a short distance, halted the troop of men-at-arms.

"Have ye the troop? And is all well?" asked Robert Sadler, his wide mouth stretched in a treacherous smile.

"Yea," responded Sir Thomas.

"Walter Skinner and Richard Wood - do they still keep watch from the tree?" asked Robert Sadler, smiling still more widely.

"Why, what is that to thee?" demanded Sir Thomas, haughtily. "It is we who do the king's business. Thou doest but ours."

"Ay," answered Robert Sadler, with feigned humility; "I do but yours."

"Thou sayest well. But think not to pry into the king's business as thou dost into the affairs at the castle. From thine own showing thou must have been a great meddler there."

"And how could I have done thy business there if I had not meddled, as thou callst it?"

"I say not that thou couldst," returned Sir Thomas. "I do but warn thee not to meddle with us. And now, where is the package?"

"Package? Package?" mumbled Robert Sadler, in apparent bewilderment.

"The package, sirrah, thou wert to deliver from Chester to her ladyship. Hast forgotten the purpose of thy journey?"

"Oh, ay, the package!" returned Robert Sadler, uneasily. "I am like to be berated by her ladyship for returning without it."

"We would not have thee so berated," said the aid, speaking for the first time. "And so I come to thine help." And he reached beneath the short cloak of Robert Sadler and drew forth the package.

"I pray thee, return it to me," said Robert Sadler, humbly. "Without it I am undone."

"Do thou but parley as thou saidst with the warder on the bridge, and thou wilt find there will be no upbraiding from her ladyship to cause thee alarm," returned the aid.

"And when wilt thou pay me the sum of money?" asked Robert Sadler, anxiously, not liking either his reception or his subsequent treatment at the hands of Sir Thomas's aid.

"And what is that to thee?" demanded Sir Thomas, fiercely. "If I withhold the sum altogether it is no more than what hath been done by mightier men than I. Do thou parley on the bridge as thou saidst, or thy head shall answer for it. Ride on now before us. We will await our opportunity in the edge of the wood."

"Thou didst not speak so to me," said the traitor, "when thou wouldst have me do this deed. It was then, 'Good Robert Sadler,' and 'I will reward thee well.' Naught didst thou say of my head answering my failure to obey thy will." Then he rode on as he had been commanded.

He now saw that he had betrayed her ladyship and her son for naught, and his dejection thereat was plainly visible. But presently he sat upright in triumph as he remembered his plan, which he had for the moment forgotten, - to betray Hugo into their hands and keep back Josceline for himself to deliver to the king. How he was to accomplish this difficult thing he did not know, but, in his ignorance, he imagined it might easily be done.

Sir Thomas and his aid were watching him. "The knave meaneth to play us false," observed the aid. "See how he sitteth and rideth in triumph."

"His head answereth for it if he doth," returned Sir Thomas, fiercely.

And now they had all arrived at the edge of the wood and the sun was down. "Set forward across the open, sirrah," commanded Sir Thomas, "and see that thou fail not in thine office."

The traitor ground his teeth in rage, but outwardly he was calm as, putting his horse to the trot, he advanced toward the great gate and wound his horn. "Now may the old warder show more than his usual caution," said Robert Sadler. "My head is likely to fall whether we get in or whether we be kept out. And it were pleasant to see these villains foiled in their desires." The old warder, obeying the instructions of William Lorimer, beyond keeping the traitor waiting a quarter of an hour, by which delay the darkness desired by William Lorimer drew so much the nearer, having answered the summons, let down the bridge with unaccustomed alacrity of motion. In accordance with the same instructions, he kept his back to the direction from which the troop were expected to come, and he seemed quite as ready to parley after the bridge was down as even Sir Thomas could have desired.

"The warder groweth doltish," observed Sir Thomas, as he prepared to set forward.

"Mayhap," answered the aid.

"What meanest thou by 'mayhap'?" demanded Sir Thomas.

But by this time the whole troop were in motion and making a rush for the bridge. They gained it; they were across it, sweeping Robert Sadler before them, and within the walls before the sluggish old warder had seemed to see what was happening. They were well across the outer court before they noticed the strange air of emptiness that seemed to have fallen on the place. They stormed into the inner court; and here, too, all was silence. And then they turned on Robert Sadler. "Art thou a double traitor?" demanded Sir Thomas.

But the vacant astonishment of Robert Sadler's face gave true answer.

"He hath been made a dupe," said the aid. "He hath been sent to Chester that the castle might be rid of him."

"Nay," returned Sir Thomas. "Thou art ever unduly suspicious." Then turning to Robert Sadler he said: "Where be the men-at-arms of the castle? Where do they hide themselves because of us? And where bideth her ladyship and her son?" Then catching sight of the open door of the stairway tower, without awaiting Robert Sadler's reply, he led the way thither and up the stair, dragging the reluctant Robert Sadler with him, and was followed by the troop.

The ladies' bower was empty. The treasure from the chests was also gone. Down the troop rushed violently, and into the great hall and out again. Everywhere silence. Darkness had now fallen, and with torches the troop of men-at-arms, led by Sir Thomas and his aid, ran about the inner court, peering into the empty stables and offices. Presently to Robert Sadler the light of a torch revealed the postern gate ajar. "They must have fled!" he cried. "See!" and he pointed to the postern gate.

"Mount and follow!" commanded Sir Thomas.

"Nay, not in the darkness," objected the aid. "Wait for the moon to rise."

"Ay, wait!" exclaimed Sir Thomas, impatiently. "I believe thou wast born with that word in thy mouth. Wouldst have them get a better start of us than they have? Dost know that they did leave the treasure chests empty, and then dost thou counsel us to wait on the tardy moon? 'Twas rich treasure they took, or report speaketh false. And every moment maketh our chance to seize it smaller."

Every man was now astride his horse, and Sir Thomas, his hand on Robert Sadler's bridle, dashed ahead. The rest followed, crowding through the narrow gate and out into the darkness on the narrow bridge. Here and there a torch gleamed, and its reflection shone full in the glassy water of the ditch. Here was no shadowy depth of a ravine, but a broad plain, - a watery plain, into which the heavily weighted horses and riders sank, rising to cry for help and catch at straws. The cries of the drowning only hurried those behind to the rescue, who, supposing their fellows in advance to be assailed, rushed headlong on to the same fate. The torches were extinguished, and none knew which way to turn to escape. So perished the whole troop, Robert Sadler going down in the grasp of Sir Thomas De Lany.

Across the moat, ready mounted to ride, were William Lorimer and the few men-at-arms left him by Lady De Aldithely on her departure. "So may it be with all traitors and thieves," said he. "And now fare we southward to France and our lord. We need not the light of the moon to show us our path."

The clatter of their horses' hoofs soon died away, and when the moon rose it shone down on the deserted castle, and on the shining water of the moat near the postern, but it shone not on horse or rider living or dead. All night William Lorimer and his little troop rode, not cautiously and shrinkingly, but boldly; and they went into camp in the early morning in Sherwood Forest, more miles away from home than Hugo and Humphrey had covered in all their journeying.

And in the swamp Walter Skinner, who had finally extricated himself from the mire, floundered about from bog to pool, and from pool to bog, vowing vengeance on Humphrey, while Hugo and the faithful serving-man, avoiding Gainsborough, pushed on toward Lincoln.

"I did dream of being taken by the constable," said Humphrey, "which betokeneth want of wit. I know not what were better to do. What sayest thou?" And he looked questioningly at Hugo.

The boy smiled. He could not help wondering if this were not the first time in his life that Humphrey had acknowledged himself at a loss what to do. A dream had caused him to doubt his own possession of sufficient wit for all purposes, - something which no amount of argument could have accomplished. But to-day Hugo felt no contempt for him. He smiled only at the one weakness which was a foil to Humphrey's many excellent qualities. And he said pleasantly, "Why, how now, Humphrey? Thou dost need another dream to restore thy courage."

Humphrey eyed him doubtfully. "Dost think so, lad?" he said. "Mayhap thou art right. But I go not in the lead till I have it. Wit is not the same at all times. Perchance something hath damaged mine for the time. Do thou lead till I recover it; for thou art no more a stranger to me as when we started."

"Nor thou to me, good Humphrey," replied Hugo, with an affectionate smile. "And I say, let us on with all courage to Lincoln."

" And why, lad? " asked Humphrey. " Because thou

wouldst see the place, even as I would see Ferrybridge a while back?"

"Partly," laughed Hugo. "And partly because it lieth very well in our way."

"Hast ever been there?" asked Humphrey, anxiously.

"Nay, but mine uncle, the prior, hath often been. And I know the place by report. We come to it by the north. Came we from the south, we could see it some twenty miles off, because the country lieth flat around it, and the city is set on a hill. Why, surely thou dost know the place. It was a city under the Danes."

"Yea, I have heard of it from my grandsire," acknowledged Humphrey; "but I know not if king's men be like to flourish there. For us that is the principal thing."

Hugo laughed. "Ah, my brave Humphrey," he said, "why shouldst thou fear king's men? Thou who canst lift up a king's man by the shoulders and plant him like a rush in the miry pool!"

At this Humphrey smiled slightly himself. "Well, lad," he said presently, "I will not gainsay thee. Go we to Lincoln, and may good come of it. But we stay not long?"

"Why, that," answered Hugo, "is what no man can tell. We must be cautious."

"Ay, lad," assented Humphrey, approvingly.

"Thou knowest of Bishop Hugh of Avalon?" inquired

Hugo, chatting of whatever came to his mind in the hope to bring back Humphrey's confidence in himself.

"Nay, lad," returned the serving-man. "I know no more of bishops than thou of hedgehogs and other creatures of the wood."

"This was a bishop, I have heard mine uncle say, that loved the birds. He hath now been nine years dead, and another man is, in his stead, bishop of Lincoln. But in his time he had many feathered pets, and one a swan, so hath mine uncle said. And also, he never feared to face the king."

"Sayest thou so, lad?" responded Humphrey, with some degree of interest. "Mayhap his spirit still may linger in the place, and so king's men not flourish there. We will on to see."

So in due time they came to the town, and entered through its old Roman gate, and, looking down the long hill on the top of which they stood, saw the city of Lincoln, which, when William the Conqueror came, had eleven hundred and fifty houses.

"It is a great place," remarked Humphrey, "and maketh a goodly show."

CHAPTER XI

In vain Richard Wood and his men had scoured the forest near Doncaster. They found no trace of those they sought. "Did I believe, like some, in witchcraft," declared Richard Wood, "so should I say there was witchcraft in their escape. Why, what should a Saxon serving-man and a boy of fourteen know, that they should foil good men on a chase?"

"Ay," responded one of his men-at-arms, "but thou seest they have done it. In this forest they are not. Mayhap they lie close in the town of Doncaster."

Richard Wood looked at him reflectively. "I had not thought on that," he said. "Mayhap thou art right. Go we into the town and see. We need rest, and bite, and sup, and the beasts also need the same."

So the weary four entered the town of Doncaster and drew rein before the Green Dragon Inn. And one of the grooms who took the horses was the same vacant-faced, foolish fellow who had received the coin from Walter Skinner. "Here be more king's men," he said to himself, "and mayhap another coin for me. I will send them also to the Isle of Axholme, where I judge sorrow hath met the other king's man, since the horseshoe had of the Evil One did come galloping back without a rider." And he smiled ingratiatingly at Richard Wood,

Gulielma Zollinger

who took no notice of him. Whereat, somewhat crestfallen, he was fain to lead the horse away, the others having been already taken care of by other grooms who had no thought of the Isle of Axholme, and no hopeful expectation of coins.

The morning that saw Hugo and Humphrey far on their way to Lincoln saw Richard Wood rise refreshed at the Green Dragon with his determination to continue the chase well renewed. And that same morning it had occurred to the vacant-faced groom that he must speak now or never if he expected any reward for his speech. So the instant Richard Wood appeared in the inn yard he sidled up to him and began, at the same time knocking his grooming tools, which he still held in his hands, nervously together, an accompaniment to his speech, which seemed to surprise the spy. "I did come from Gainsborough two nights agone," he said.

"That is naught to me, varlet," interrupted Richard Wood. "Get thee back to thy grooming."

"Yea, verily," insisted the groom; "but it is somewhat to thee," and he knocked the tools together in his hands at a great rate. "I did come by the Isle of Axholme. And the other king's man did accuse me of drunkenness and revellings when I did begin to have speech with him of the matter, but he did change his mind, and give me a coin. Do thou but the same and thou also mayest hear what I did see."

Richard Wood regarded him attentively. "Speak truth," he said, "and say that I would hear, and thou shalt have two coins."

The vacant-faced groom grinned a broad and foolish

grin. "Said I not," he cried joyfully, "that thou wert a better man than the other? For he was but small and fierce and hath met sorrow, or his horse had not come back riderless."

Richard Wood smiled contemptuously at this reference to Walter Skinner. Then he said: "Thou didst come by the Isle of Axholme. What sawest thou there?"

"Why, thou canst talk like an advocate," said the foolish groom, who had never seen an advocate in his life. "Ay," he continued, "he that giveth two coins is ever a better master than he that giveth one. And I did see a young lord and his serving-man lie on a bed of rushes; and ever and anon the serving-man did rise to feed the blazing fire of reeds; and it was the fire I first did see, and, going to the fire, I did see them."

"The Isle of Axholme lieth eighteen miles long and five in breadth," said Richard Wood. "Where didst thou see them?" and he held up three coins.

"Toward the south end on a little solid place which hath on it three scrubby trees. There did they lie." And the groom left off speaking to eye the money in ecstasy, for not often did such wealth come his way.

Richard Wood tossed him the coins. "Make haste with the horses," he said. "Hast thou no other marks to know the place?"

"Why, nay," answered the groom, regretfully. "But thou wilt surely know it when thou comest to it," and he smiled broadly.

Ten minutes later the party was off, and, crossing the

Gulielma Zollinger

Don at the town, found themselves in the Isle of Axholme. And then Richard Wood paused to give his men instructions. "Here do we need caution," he said. "This fellow is not easily to be caught, for I make naught of the young lord. He is doubtless some trusty retainer sent with the lad by her ladyship because he hath wit to hide and double on his track and so baffle pursuit. But he hath not yet reached port to set sail for France, and mayhap he will not. It remaineth now for us to hide and creep among the rushes and reeds and scrubby trees, and so come up with him unseen."

The men-at-arms listened respectfully, and the party separating themselves so that each man rode alone at a little distance from his fellows, they took the same general direction, and so advanced slowly and carefully, taking advantage of every bit of cover in their way, and often pausing to listen. They had proceeded in this manner some two hours when Richard Wood saw the three scrub trees, and, waving the signal to his men, the advance was made with renewed caution. At last all were near enough to see the couch of rushes and the ashes of the fire, but they saw nothing of serving-man or boy, who by this time had reached Lincoln. Silently, at a signal from Richard Wood, the party drew together. "Ye see," said he, pointing to the place, "that they be not here. Either they be gone roaming about for the day in search of food, or they be gone altogether. We may not know of a surety till evening when, if they be not altogether gone, they will return. If they be gone, we have lost a day and given them an added start of us. Wherefore I counsel that we pursue the search warily through the Isle in the hope that we come up with them. What say ye?"

"We say well," responded the men.

The party now separated again, and, going even more slowly than before through the silent Isle, sought to be as noiseless as possible. But every now and then some horse splashed suddenly and heavily into a pool, or scrambling out of the water crunched and broke the reeds and scared the water-fowl, which rose shrieking and flew noisily away. At such mishaps Richard Wood restrained his impatience as well as he was able, knowing that they were unavoidable and that his men were faithful. Thus another hour went by and there was no trace of the fugitives. They were now going due northwest, and a half-hour later one of the men-at-arms gave the signal. Silently Richard Wood approached him. "I did see one of them," said the man in a low tone. "He lieth beneath a tree beyond this fringe of reeds on the next solid place."

And now Richard Wood was all excitement. "Which was it?" he asked; "the young lord or the serving-man?"

"Why, thou knowest I did never see either," replied the man, "and I could not draw very near. But the person I did see did seem too small to be the stout Saxon serving-man of whom thou hast spoken."

Without a word, but with his face expressing great triumph, Richard Wood waved to the others to approach, which they did slowly and with care. Having come up with him, he communicated to them the news he had received, and, bidding them scatter in such a manner as to surround the little place on which the fortunate man-at-arms had discovered the man or boy lying, he waited with such patience as he could muster until the time had elapsed necessary for the carrying out of his commands, and then advanced to capture the young lord with his own hands. And what was his disgust, when he came up with the sleeper under the tree, to find Walter Skinner.

"And is it thou, Walter Skinner?" he demanded when he had roused him. "And what doest thou here?"

"Ay, Richard Wood, it is I. And what I do here is no concern of thine. Here have I been a day and a night and this second day. Little have I had to eat, and my drinking-horn is but now empty. And I have been planted in a miry pool. And I have lost my horse and my way also; and have floundered into more bogs and out of them than can be found in all Robert Sadler's Ireland. Were I king, I would have no Isle of Axholme in all my dominions. Could I do no better, I would pull down the hill of Lincoln and cart it hither to fill these vile water-holes. Do but see my doublet and hose. Were I called suddenly to the palace would not the king and the court despise me as a drunken ruffler from some revel-rout that had fallen from his horse? When all the blame is to be laid on this Isle of Axholme, which ought, by right, to belong to France, since it is full of frogs."

"Thou art crazed, as thou always art when thou drinkest," said Richard Wood, coldly.

"Dost thou say I have been drinking?" demanded Walter Skinner, starting up.

"Yea, I say it. Thou sayest it also. For thou didst say thy drinking-horn was but now empty."

"Yea, verily," answered Walter Skinner. "If thou be a true man do but fill it for me again. Or lead me from this vile place, where one heareth naught but the squawk of birds and the croak of frogs. I would fain see the Green Dragon and the idiot groom that did send me here. I warrant thee I will crack his pate for him."

"Where is thy horse?" asked Richard Wood.

"Ay, where is he? Who but that vile serving-man did bid the young lord cut him loose?"

"Thou dreamest," said Richard Wood, incredulously. "Would a serving-man forget his station and bid his master do a task?"

"Ay, would he, if he were this serving-man. I tell thee he would bid the king himself do a task if he chose, and, moreover, the king would obey. 'Twas he did plant me in the miry pool and say I did dance well but somewhat slowly when I did try to unplant myself, and for every foot I took up sunk the other deeper in the mire. And he did dub me 'Sir Stick-in-the-Mud,' moreover, for which I do owe him a grudge and will requite him. I will meet him one day where there be no miry pools, and then let him beware." This last he uttered with a look which was intended to be fierce, but which was only silly.

"Didst thou come after them alone with no man to help thee?" asked Richard Wood, still more incredulously.

"Oh, I did have help enough," was the answer, with a crafty look. "I did have to my help a yew bow with a silken string that the king himself need not despise, and a great store of arrows, moreover. And I did hide and bide my time until the darkness of night came and the fire blazed high. And then I did let my arrows fly.

Gulielma Zollinger

And what did the serving-man? He did catch up the very fire and rush upon me. And later he did break my arrows and cut my bow-string, and fling my bow into the water, and then departed, I know not where."

"Thou art but a sorry fool," declared Richard Wood, after some thought. "And yet I cannot find it in my heart to leave thee here. Mount up behind me, and at Gainsborough I will set thee down. There canst thou shift for thyself, and chase or forbear to chase as thou choosest."

"Ay, thou sayest truly," said the half-drunken Walter Skinner. "And should I now forbear to chase, a dukedom would no more than reward me for the perils I have seen. First in the lofty tree watching the castle; and thou knowest that now, when, from the interdict, no bells may ring to disperse the tempests, I might have died from the lightning stroke, not once but many times. For there might have been a tempest and lightning every day, and no thanks to the king that there was not. Then, too, I did encounter perils from the boughs which might have broken and did not. And wherefore did they not? Because they were too tough and sound. And this, too, moreover, was no thanks to the king. And two horses have I lost, - one mine own and one the gift of the prior of St. Edmund's. And did the prior wish to give me the beast? Nay, he did not, and would have refused it if he had dared. He made as if he gave it because of the king, but he did not. He feared before me, as well he might. For I had met a hedgehog, and when a man is in such a case he is in no mind to have a horse refused him by a fat prior. And all this also was no thanks to the king. And then I did meet that varlet of a groom at the Green Dragon, and he did send me here. And here have I met such misfortunes as would last a man his lifetime."

To all this Richard Wood had lent but half an ear, being occupied in turning over in his mind the fact that Hugo and Humphrey had been in the Isle and had gone, and trying to decide what was best to do. He now looked at him. "Mount up behind me and cease thy prating," he said. Then turning to the men-at-arms he continued: "We go hence to Gainsborough. From thence down to Sherwood Forest. It seemeth this serving man loveth woods and wilds. Therefore it were waste of time to seek for him in towns and beaten ways."

All the while he was speaking Walter Skinner, with many groans, was trying to mount behind his old companion; but, on account of the horse shying his objections to such a proceeding, and the drunken clumsiness of Walter Skinner himself, nothing had been accomplished. Richard Wood therefore called on one of the men-at-arms to dismount and hoist him up; which he did much as if the fierce little spy had been a bag of meal, and much to Walter Skinner's discomfort, who suddenly found himself heavily seated with one leg doubled up under him and with a bumped face where he had struck against Richard Wood's shoulder. He soon righted himself, however, and, clinging to his old friend, rode away to Gainsborough.

CHAPTER XII

As Hugo and Humphrey with Fleetfoot in leash looked about them from the backs of their horses, it suddenly occurred to the prudent serving-man that to go to an inn was not the safest thing in the world for them to do. "Thou art like our young lord Josceline, and Josceline is like his father," said Humphrey. "And though they be few who would aid the king against my lord now fled away to France, still there be a few unprincipled knaves in every place. And though Lincoln had no longer ago than nine years the good Hugh thou didst speak of for its bishop, still, if some knave abiding here should look upon thee and say, 'Behold the son of De Aldithely! I will take him!' it might go ill with thee. Wherefore I know not what were best to do. We be now come here, and have no place to lay our heads. The woods and the fens be safer."

Then Hugo smiled. "Thou speakest not of thyself, Humphrey," he said. "How if some knave abiding here should think to take not only the son of De Aldithely, but his brave serving-man also? Thou art more careful of me than of thyself, and I shall call it to mind one day."

"Ay, lad," said Humphrey, smiling in his turn. "Thou art as brave as any De Aldithely thyself. For who but the brave taketh time to think of another, and he only a serving-man, when himself is in danger? But all this talk procureth us no safe place to lie, and methinks already there be some in the streets that gape upon us."

"No more than idlers ever do," responded Hugo, with assurance. "We be two strangers, and Fleetfoot, moreover, is a fine hound and worth the looking at."

"Ay," said Humphrey, regretfully. "The hound is yet likely to get us into trouble. But whither do we go? I would fain be out of the sight of these gazers."

"Not to an inn, good Humphrey. I have here a ring from mine uncle, the prior, which, when I show it at certain places, will procure us lodging, and Lincoln is one of them. We go not down the hill toward the river. Our place is here near the cathedral in the house of the canon Richard Durdent."

Humphrey smiled. "It is good that thou hast for thine uncle a prior," he said.

"Ay," responded Hugo. "He is a kind uncle. Where I show his ring I get not only lodging, but certain moneys to help me on my way. He thought it not best that I should travel far with much gold about me, wherefore he hath made these arrangements. He knoweth the canon Durdent of old."

"I would see this ring," said Humphrey, curiously.

"And so thou shalt," promised Hugo, "when we be safely lodged."

"How far reacheth the ring?" inquired Humphrey.

"Even to France," was the reply.

"Then I would that thou wouldst trust it in my keeping," said Humphrey, earnestly.

The boy looked at him; once more he beheld him rushing upon the spy in the Isle of Axholme; once more heard his indignant cry, "And wouldst thou slay my dear lad?" His eyes shone, but all he said was, "I will trust thee with the custody of the ring, Humphrey, save at such times as I must have it to show."

The serving-man smiled well pleased, though he said nothing; for there was no time for words, since they had already come to the door of the house they sought.

"The ring is a powerful one," said Humphrey, when they had been well received and lodged. "I would fain see it."

Hugo smiled and handed it to him. The serving-man took it in his large hand and regarded it narrowly. "After all it is but a carved fish on a red stone," he said.

"Thou dost not ask what it betokeneth?"

Humphrey glanced up quickly. "Thou canst make merry over my dreams," he said, "and what they betoken. And here thou comest with a circlet of gold crowned with a red stone having the likeness of a fish on it. And thou sayest it betokeneth somewhat. Thou mayest no more deride my dreams."

"Nay, nay, my good Humphrey," laughed the boy. "Thou shalt have thy dreams if thou wilt. But my uncle's priory is dedicated to St. Wilfrid, who taught the Sussex people to catch all fish, when before they knew only how to catch eels. Therefore my uncle putteth a fish on the ring, that whosoever of his friends that seeth it may know it is the ring of Roger Aungerville, prior of St. Wilfrid's."

"So doth the fish of thine uncle give us lodging and safety," observed Humphrey, thoughtfully. "It is a good ring. I will hold it with all care." And he drew forth the small pouch of gold pieces which Lady De Aldithely had given him, and put the ring carefully inside it. "It hangeth about my neck, thou seest," he said, as he replaced the pouch, "and no man may take it unless he first taketh my head."

"Or disableth thee with an arrow or a sword thrust," said Hugo.

"Ay," answered Humphrey, gravely. "I had not spoken of arrows and sword thrusts. I have the hope that we may meet with neither. And though the way is long when one must creep and hide and crawl, and go to the south one day, to the southwest another, and the southeast another, yet the end cometh at last, and I have hope it be a good end. And now I ask thee how long we bide and whence go we from here? Doth the ring decide?"

"Nay," replied Hugo. "Thou shalt have thy share of the making of plans. But I would fain learn what we may of the region round about, and of the safety or danger it holdeth for us ere we sally forth."

"Why, now," said Humphrey, approvingly, "thou art learning craft. For who but a fool would be careless of danger? Thou art like my lord, who knoweth when to

Gulielma Zollinger

strike and when to flee. And for that it is that his men follow him madly in battle. For, if there be risk, they do know it to be necessary risk, with a certain gain to be obtained at the end of it, if all go well. But if there be no gain in view, my lord leadeth them not into unnecessary danger, and so it is that he is a power and the king hateth him. Thou doest well to look ahead of thee, for there is no gain to be had from lying in the king's dungeon, but mayhap thou shalt lose thy head also, as well as thy liberty. But what doest thou now?"

"Why, I fain would sleep, having had no rest in the night. But the canon knoweth naught of that, nor may I tell him. He must be busy till even, and so he sendeth me to view the cathedral; and thou mayest go with me."

To this Humphrey made no reply, but followed his young master in silence.

The verger who took them in charge was an ancient man called Paulinus of Mansfield, having been born in that place. And he soon saw that what he had to show of the unfinished cathedral was lost on the heavy-lidded boy who was half asleep, and upon the Saxon serving-man, who felt no interest in such matters. Wherefore when he came from the chapter-house into the cloisters he, being old and feeble, was fain to sit down on a stone bench and rest; and he motioned Hugo to a seat beside him.

Humphrey had the idea that, at all times and in all places, wisdom was with the aged. Besides, the old verger reminded him, in certain particulars, of his own grandsire, who was a great talker and who knew more of all matters concerning the countryside than half a dozen other men.

And he now cast such an expressive glance upon Hugo and gave such a meaning nod toward Paulinus, that the boy must perforce have understood, even if he had not added in a tone too low to catch the somewhat deaf ears of the old man, "Ask him what thou wouldest know."

At once Hugo threw off his drowsiness and, in the most pleasing manner he could summon, requested to be informed of the surrounding district.

"It is easy to see thou art a stranger," said the gratified old man. "And thou wouldest know the region round about Lincoln?" he repeated. "Thou hast come to him who can tell thee of it, for I was born and brought up in these parts. It is truly a noble region on all sides save the east, where lieth the fen country. For here cometh the king frequently to take his pleasure. And that is oft pleasure to him which would be none to gentler minds."

At this Hugo turned startled eyes on Humphrey, who stood at a little distance, but who did not appear to notice his look.

"Hast ever seen the king?" inquired Paulinus.

"Nay," replied Hugo.

"Nor need thou wish so to do," returned the aged Paulinus. "I speak to thee in confidence, for surely thou art a worthy youth or thou wouldest not be guest to the Canon Durdent. The king is the youngest and the worst son of the wicked Queen Eleanor of Aquitaine, who is now, by the mercy of God, dead. I could tell thee tales of the king's cruelty that would affright thee, but I will not. He loveth to hunt in the Forest of Sherwood, and therefore hath he castles and lodges hereabout, which he doth frequent as it pleaseth him. And he hath ever had a liking for that castle at Newark which our bishop of Lincoln, Alexander the Magnificent, did build. I could tell thee tales of the dungeons there - knowest thou what they be like?" And he paused and looked at Hugo, who was somewhat pale, for the word "dungeon" had come to have a fearsome meaning to him.

"Nay," answered the boy, "I know not."

"Thou goest in the castle through a passage to the northwest corner, where is a door which is guarded. Here is the solid rock; and inside that door be two dungeons scooped out of it. No stair descendeth to them. Those who occupy them at the king's will are lowered into them by a rope, and there is no chance by which they may escape. There they abide in darkness, and no skill, or cunning, or bravery can avail them so that they may escape." The old man paused.

Presently Hugo asked, "And where lieth this castle from here?"

"It lieth to the southwest, less than a score of miles away."

Hugo said nothing, and, after a short silence, Paulinus began again: "If thou shouldest journey hence a little south of west, then wouldest thou come to Clipstone Palace, which lieth not far from Mansfield, where I was born. Here the king doth sometimes frequent, and from thence he goeth to hunt in the forest. But better men than he have frequented it when his father, King Henry, and his brother, King Richard, did sojourn there. Thinkest thou to journey that way?"

"Nay," replied Hugo. "Methinks our way lieth not toward Clipstone."

"Mayhap it were better to journey by Newark, where be the dungeons I have told thee of; and so, when thou hast viewed that castle, journey on southward to Nottingham, where the king hath another castle which oft holdeth many prisoners. He keepeth there certain children, the hostages he demandeth of their fathers. And no man knoweth when they will die, for that is a matter of the king's pleasure."

The old verger now seemed to fall into a reverie, in which he remained so long that Hugo rose from the stone bench, thus rousing him. Slowly he raised himself from his seat, having apparently forgotten all that he had just been saying, and conducted them to the entrance, where he bade them adieu.

"I fear to bide here longer," said Humphrey, as they returned to the canon's house. "Let us away to the fens on the east of this place, and, through their wilds, make our way southward."

Hugo reflected. Then he answered, "Thou art right, Humphrey. It were not best to journey so near the king's castles and dungeons. We will away to-morrow morn to the fens."

This, however, they were unable to do. The canon desired not to part with his friend's nephew so soon.

Seeing which, Humphrey consoled himself for the delay by buying ample stores of provisions, with which he so loaded the horses that the canon wondered. "There be towns all the way from hence to London, and inns in all the towns," he said. "Thou mayest journey without that packhorse load."

But Humphrey was obstinate. "The goods be bought," he said stubbornly.

The canon who knew not that they intended to travel through the fens and avoid the towns, looked pityingly at Hugo. "I see thou hast a master in thy man," he observed. "I wonder thine Uncle Roger did not choose for thee a more obedient servant."

It was on the tip of the boy's tongue to tell him that his uncle's prudence had furnished him with no servant at all. But, at a warning glance from Humphrey, he kept silence. And then, with the blessing of the canon, they set out down the hill through the narrow street toward the river, which they crossed and found themselves outside the town.

CHAPTER XIII

Having deposited Walter Skinner before the door of the Lion in Gainsborough, Richard Wood and his men set off for Sherwood Forest in the strong hope of coming up with the runaways they sought. And, in nowise cast down by his recent discouraging experiences, Walter Skinner held his head high and looked around him fiercely, as of yore. His doublet and hose besplashed with mud and torn by briers seemed not to give him any concern; neither did the condition of his shoes, which were foul with the slimy mud of the swamp.

"I will have breakfast, sirrah, and that immediately," he said to the waiter when he had entered the inn.

The waiter eyed him doubtfully.

"Make haste. I command thee to it. Dally not with me. I serve the king," said the fierce little man, loftily.

"Thy service hath taken thee in strange paths," observed the innkeeper, who had drawn near.

"Not so strange as thine will take thee in if thou delay me," retorted Walter Skinner, haughtily.

There was in the bar a strange man of a crafty and evil

face, and he now drew near the imperious little spy, and humbly besought the honor of taking his breakfast in Walter Skinner's company.

"And so thou shalt," said the spy, condescendingly. "And mayhap, since I have lost my horse, thou canst direct me where I can find another. I have no time to go harrying a prior for one."

The landlord now led the way obsequiously, and soon the strange pair were seated in one of the several private rooms of the inn, with the promise that breakfast should be served to them at once.

Then said the stranger: "As to the matter of a horse, I have at this moment one by me which I would fain dispose of. He is not gentle enough to my liking."

"I care not for gentleness in a horse," declared Walter Skinner. "I warrant thee I can ride the beast whether he be gentle or not."

"Thou lookest a bold rider," observed the stranger, craftily.

"He that doeth the king's business hath need to be a bold rider," returned Walter Skinner, with a look which was intended to convey the information that he could unfold mysteries were he so disposed.

"Thou art high in the king's counsels, then?" asked the stranger, with a covert smile.

"Not so high but I shall be higher when I have finished the business in hand," returned Walter Skinner, patronizingly. The breakfast being now brought he said no more, but ate like a starving man, and with a very unfavorable memory of his late meals of wild berries in the swamp. The crafty-eyed stranger ate more sparingly, and seemed to be mentally measuring the fierce little man opposite him. At last he asked, "And whence goest thou from here?"

"What is that to thee?" demanded Walter Skinner. "Wouldst thou pry into the king's business? Reach me the bottle."

The stranger obeyed, and after taking a long drink Walter Skinner said: "I will now tell thee what I would not tell to every man. First, from here I go to the Green Dragon at Doncaster, there to crack the pate of the groom that did send me into the Isle of Axholme, where I did have all sorts of contumely heaped upon me. And after that I shall pursue my course or not, as it pleaseth me. Richard Wood did give me permission so to do. Knowest thou Richard Wood?"

"Nay," answered the stranger.

"He is well enough in his place, and that is in the high tree overlooking the castle. But when he will ride abroad with men-at-arms behind him to obey his word, then he thinketh that he may tell me also, his old friend, what I may and may not do. He hath even bid me cease prating. What thinkest thou of such a man?"

"Why, he must be a bold man that would bid thee cease prating," replied the stranger.

Walter Skinner took another drink and then looked long and earnestly at him. "Thou art a man of reason," he said; "yea, and of wisdom, moreover. And come, now, show me thy ungentle horse. I promise thee I will back him or - or - " He did not finish his sentence, and the two went out to the inn yard, where stood a horse which did not seem to be particularly vicious. And the animal was soon in the possession of the spy for a very fair sum in exchange.

"I will but fix his bridle for thee," said the man, "while thou payest the reckoning, and then mayest thou ride with speed and safety. I may not stay to see thee go, for I must instantly depart."

"Ay, thou hast a hard master, no doubt," observed Walter Skinner, with a shake of the head.

"Necessity is my master," said the stranger.

"Ay, ay, no doubt," returned Walter Skinner, going toward the bar. "Necessity is not mine, however."

A half-hour later, when the spy was ready to set out, the stranger had disappeared. But he did not miss him, for the landlord himself had come out into the yard to see him off, while all the grooms stood about, and two or three maids looked on.

"Good people, give back," said Walter Skinner, grandly. "Block not the way of the king's man. Ye mean well and kindly, no doubt, but I would have ye withdraw yourselves a little space."

By the help of a groom he was mounted, and a moment later he was out of the inn yard. But now a strange thing happened. He was no sooner out of the town than the horse refused to be controlled. In vain the little spy tried to head him toward Doncaster. The stranger had removed the bit, putting in its place a wisp of straw, which the horse quickly chewed to pieces, and then, with a shake of the head, he galloped off to the south.

"Thou beast!" cried the spy. "What meanest thou? Thou art held in by bit and bridle. Dost not know it?"

It seemed that the horse did not, for he went on at a faster pace.

"Thou art worse than the prior's horse!" cried Walter Skinner, dropping the reins and clinging round the animal's neck. "I would I had the stranger that did sell thee to me! I would crack his pate also, even as I will the pate of the groom at the Green Dragon."

Giving no heed to the remonstrances of his rider or the unevenness of the road, the horse kept on until he entered the gates of Lincoln, and stopped before the Swan with a loud and joyous neigh.

At the sound two grooms ran out. "Here he be!" cried one. "Here be Black Tom that was stole but two nights agone," cried the other; while in great amazement Walter Skinner sat up and gazed from one to the other.

"What meanest thou, sirrah?" he demanded of the second groom. "Sayest thou a horse is stolen when I did pay good money for him but this morning? And, moreover, who would steal such a beast that will mind not the bridle and only runs his course the faster for the spur?"

"Ay, thou knewest not that he was stolen, no doubt," retorted the second groom, sarcastically. "But here cometh master, who will soon pull thee down from thy high perch, thou little minute of a dirty man. Thou hast slept in the swamp over night, I do be bound, and now comest to brave it out, seeing thou canst not make way with the horse."

"I would have thee know, villain, that I serve the king, and did buy the horse in Gainsborough this morn to replace the one which the young lord did cut loose. And whether I did sleep in the swamp or in a duke's chamber is naught to thee or to thy master. I have been so shaken up this morn over thy rough roads and by thy vile beast of a horse that thou and thy master shall pay for it. What! is the servant of the king to be sent into the Isle of Axholme by an idiot groom at the Green Dragon? And, being there, is he to be planted in the mire like a rush by a Saxon serving-man? And is his horse to be cut loose by the young lord at the word of that same Saxon serving-man? And is he to be carried behind Richard Wood to Gainsborough? And is he there to buy a black horse from a vile stranger? And is he to be run away with to this place when he would fain go elsewhere about his master's business, which is to catch this young lord and the Saxon serving-man? And then is he to be looked at as if he were a thief? Thou shalt repent, and so I tell thee; yea, in sackcloth and ashes. And if thou canst find no sackcloth, then thou shalt have a double portion of ashes, ye knaves, and so I promise you."

At these words the innkeeper and the grooms looked at each other. And then the innkeeper said civilly that he and the grooms had meant no offence, but that the horse had certainly been stolen from the Swan two nights before. The second groom, equally desirous with his master to conciliate, pressed forward to show him how the bit had been removed by the rascal who sold the horse so that he would come straight home again.

"Which I did but now discover," said the second groom.

And the first groom, not to be outdone, said: "If thou really seekest the young lord and the Saxon serving-man we can put thee on their track, for surely they did leave here but some three hours agone."

Walter Skinner stared stupidly for a moment, while the innkeeper reproved the groom for being beforehand with him in giving the intelligence. Then the little spy sat up straighter and put on a haughtier air than ever. "Aha, Fortune!" he cried, "thou art bound to make a duke of me whether I will or not." Then turning to the innkeeper he said: "I will enter thine inn, and do thou see that dinner be promptly served. I will then procure a change of raiment. I will then sleep over night. I will then breakfast. I will then take thy Black Tom, which I did buy, and withhold him from me if thou darest. And I will then set out after the young lord and the serving-man. I have now given thee my confidence, which if thou betray thou shalt answer for it. Why, they cannot escape me. Hath Richard Wood come up with them three several times, as I now have? Nay. If he had he would have captured them, which showeth that I be the abler man of the two; for, while I have not captured them, he hath not even caught sight of them. And now make haste with the dinner."

All this time the spy had kept his seat on the horse. He now came down, and the innkeeper, without a word, led the way to a private room, while the grooms exchanged glances. "Yon be a madman," said the first, whose name was Elfric.

"Yea, or a drunken man, which is the same thing," responded the second.

"He will catch not the young lord," declared Elfric.

"I did not dream they fled as they rode down the street to the river," observed the second. "They did go slowly enough, and the young lord looked about him curiously and unafraid."

"By that thou mayest know he was a lord, and this drunken fool speaketh true," returned Elfric. "The better the blood, the less of fear; so hath my grandsire said."

Though Walter Skinner had commanded the innkeeper and the grooms to keep what he called his confidence on pain of his vengeance, what he had said flew abroad. And wherever the little spy appeared that afternoon he seemed to arouse much curiosity. "The king must be put to it for help when he employcth such a one," commented a cooper.

"Tut, man!" was the reply. "What careth the king who doeth his pleasure so it be done? It looketh not like to be done, though, with this man for the doer of it. Why, who but a fool seeing those he sought had three good hours the start of him would give them four and twenty more?"

The cooper shrugged his shoulders. "I tell thee, Peter of the forge," he said, "that I care not if the king's will be never done, for it is a bad will. Therefore the more fools like yon he setteth to do it the better."

Meanwhile the innkeeper was thinking ruefully of the guest he had on his hands. "I may not anger him," he said to Elfric, the groom.

"Nor needest thou," replied Elfric.

"Talk not to me," said the innkeeper, impatiently. "Wouldst have me lose Black Tom? For whether he did pay the thief for him or not, he most certainly did not pay me. And thou knowest the value of Black Tom."

"Yea," answered Elfric, "I know it. But why shouldst thou lose Black Tom?"

"Why? Art thou gone daft? Didst thou hear him bid me refuse him the beast if I dared? This it is to have a bad king who will set such knaves upon his business."

"If there be but one black horse in Lincoln," replied Elfric, "thou doest well to fret. But if there be Black Dick that is broken-winded and hath the spring-halt so that he be not worth more than one day's reckoning at the Swan at the most; and if he looketh tolerably fair; and if thou mayst buy him for a small sum; and if this drunken fool knoweth not one horse from another; why needst thou worry?"

The face of the innkeeper at once cleared. "The fraud is justifiable," he said. "For why should he take my Black Tom and give me naught? I do but protect myself when I give him instead Black Dick."

"Ay, and thou doest no unfriendly turn to the young lord neither. I have been to inquire, and there be those that say he is son to De Aldithely. And doubtless he fleeth away to his brave father in France. I did think he had a familiar look this morn. And when I heard, I did repent that the Swan had put this knave upon his track. But with Black Dick he cometh not up with him in a hurry."

That night Walter Skinner found the Swan a most pleasant abiding-place, where all were attentive to serve him. "Thou hast me for thy friend," he told the innkeeper as he supped with him. "Thou hast me, I say, and not Richard Wood. And I will speak a good word for thee to the king. Not now, indeed, for it were not seemly that I should introduce thy matters until I had brought mine own to a happy issue. But what sayest thou? To pursue a young lord for many miles and capture him, - single-handed, - were that not worth a dukedom? I have here this good yew bow with a silken string and a goodly store of arrows. Oh, I will capture him, if ever I come up with him. The serving-man cutteth not this silken string nor breaketh these arrows, I warrant thee."

And, clad in his new raiment, Walter Skinner sat back in his chair and gazed pompously around.

The innkeeper listened, and, supper being over, he sought Elfric, to whom he related what had passed. "I would not that a hair of the young son of De Aldithely should be harmed," he said. "And what I dare not do, that thou must perform."

"And what is that?" asked Elfric.

"Thou must fray his bow-string so it will not be true, and thou must injure his arrows likewise."

"Right willingly will I do so," promised Elfric. "If he hit any mark he aim at when I am done with the bow and arrows, then am I as great a knave as he. And the damage shall be so small that he may not see it neither."

Gulielma Zollinger

CHAPTER XIV

Although there were those who had looked upon Hugo and Humphrey curiously in the streets of Lincoln, there were none sufficiently interested to observe what direction they took after they had left the town. And none saw them leave the road and betake themselves to the fens as safer for their journey. So east of the heights, which, to the east of Lincoln, extend in a southeasterly direction, they rode, picking their way as they might, and hopeful that now all enemies were thrown off their track.

"It is a weariness to be pursued so many days," said Hugo. "I would fain breathe easily once more."

"Ay, lad," returned Humphrey. "But that is what cannot be done in this world. When thou art forty years old, as I am, thou wilt see that every man hath his enemies and every bird and beast also, as we may perchance see in this wild fen country. It is good, therefore, to breathe as easily as one can and think no more about it. Knowest thou what these fens be like?"

"Nay; but mine uncle hath told me that they be vast, and that here and there half-wild people live in huts along the reedy shores; and that south lieth the goodly town of Peterborough, as well as the abbey of Crowland."

"Doth the ring avail at Peterborough?"

"Yea, if I have need; but there will be none." And he glanced with a smile at the heavily loaded horses they rode, and bethought himself of his plentiful supply of gold pieces. "What hast thou in all these bags and packs, Humphrey?" he asked.

"Why, the answer to that question is not so simple," was the reply. "I did but buy somewhat of all I saw, and did bestow it the best I could, so as to leave room for our legs on the sides of the horses. Should the spy pursue us, he would soon come up with us, for flee we could not, so loaded down. But I look not for him. No doubt he still lodgeth in the Isle of Axholme, and the other spy we have not of late heard from. If we but keep clear of beaten paths, we be safe enough. I will hope to have a dream to-night."

Hugo did not reply; he was looking about him in much enjoyment. The day chanced to be clear, and as far as he could see lay the level of the fen-lands. Here were trees, some straight, others leaning over the water; there were islands of reeds, and yonder the water shimmering on its shallow, winding way, so sluggish as to be almost stagnant. The whole region was alive with sound, - the cries of water-fowl, the songs of birds, and the croak of frogs. And when he rode along the water's brink, an occasional fin flashed out. Humphrey watched him with approval. "Ay, lad," he said, "thou wilt soon be wise in fen lore, for thou hast a heart to it. I will tell thee now that I have wherewith to fish in one of these same packs. Mine ears were not idle in the town, and I did learn that perch and red-eye and roach and bream frequent the waters of the fen."

"And didst thou ask what fish were in the fen?" asked Hugo, in alarm.

"Nay, lad, most surely not. But when I did see fish for sale I did praise their beauty, and they that had them did of themselves tell me where they did catch them. There be more ways of finding out things than by asking of questions."

They were now come to a small, grassy isle fringed with reeds. "Here do we get down," said Humphrey. "I would fain see if we do not catch some of those same fish for our dinner. And here is grass, moreover, where the horses can graze."

Slowly and carefully boy and man disengaged themselves from the baggage that almost encased them and dismounted. "If thou dost get a dream to-night, Humphrey," said Hugo, laughingly, "I hope thou wilt discover what we shall do with all this stuff."

"I dream not to find out such a thing as that," returned the serving-man, good-naturedly.

The horses were soon tied out, and the fishing-lines and hooks unpacked. Then Humphrey, going out on a fallen log which was half submerged, carefully plumbed the water to see how deep it was, while Hugo watched him in wonder. Next he took from another package some ground bait consisting of meal, and balls made of bread and grain, worked up in the hand. This he threw into the water, which here but two feet deep. Then in a whisper he said, "All this I did learn in Lincoln." And he bade Hugo hold his line so that the bait on the hook was about an inch from the bottom.

Hugo obeyed, and in a moment was rewarded with a red-eye about a foot long. At the same time Humphrey drew out another. And before long they had half a dozen each, for the red-eye was always sure to be one of a crowd, and it was so greedy that it took the bait readily.

"No more to-day," said Humphrey, winding up his line, "for we already have more than we can eat, and I hold it sin to slay what we cannot eat. This was I taught by my grandsire, who ever said that evil was sure to befall those who did so. And I would we could put the life back into half we have taken; but they did bite so readily that we had too many suddenly. Still, if we eat naught to speak of but fish, we may make away with most and so be spared evil."

While Humphrey dressed the too numerous fish, Hugo sought sufficient fuel to cook them, and came back to find the serving-man well satisfied. "Even as I did begin to dress the fish," he said, "there came a sound of wings, and I looked up and did behold a glede. And I did cease to move; so came he nearer, and did snatch a fish. Then came another and did snatch a fish. In quietness I did wait. Then came the first glede back and did take a fish, and the second did like-wise. And, by waiting with patience, the gledes did take two more. And now we have but six fish, and no evil will befall us, for those we can eat."

Hugo smiled, for the big serving-man had spoken with the faith of a child.

Their noon rest taken, they went on again toward the south and came by nightfall to what Humphrey decided to be a suitable place to pass the night. "I mean

Gulielma Zollinger

not," he said, "that the place would please me were we out of the fen. But being in the fen, why, there be worse places than this to be found; for it is not a bog nor a slough, and there be reeds in plenty near by."

"Do we make a fire?" asked Hugo, mindful of their experience in the Isle of Axholme.

"Yea," answered the serving-man. "If we make the fire perchance some evil person seeth us, perchance not. If we make not the fire, the chill of the fen doth get into our bones. Seest thou how the mist arises? And we be not like the holy hermits of these haunts to withstand chill and vapors."

Hugo looked at him in surprise. "How knowest thou of holy hermits?" he asked.

"I did even learn of them in Lincoln. It was the canon's servant who did tell me of St. Guthlac and St. Godric. He did know more of the holy hermits than of his master's service, I warrant thee. And that is an evil knowledge for a servant that bids him talk to the neglect of his master's good."

The fire alight, the two lay down, Hugo to fall asleep and Humphrey to rise at intervals through the night and throw on reeds that so the fen mists might work no harm to the boy, to whom he was now as devotedly attached as ever he was to Josceline. The morning's breakfast was from the packs which Humphrey acknowledged were too full for prudent carrying; and by the time Walter Skinner arose at the Swan they were off again, still southward. They were now nearer the coast, and a great fen eagle flew screaming over their heads. "To dream that eagles do fly over your head doth betoken evil fortune," remarked Humphrey, gravely. "But I think we need not fear those eagles which do not fly in dreams."

And now in the yard of the Swan all was astir. Elfric had taken Black Dick out and gently exercised him so that his spring-halt need not be at once apparent, and there was no little anxiety on the part of the host to get rid of his guest expeditiously. The spy, however, with his usual dulness, did not perceive it, but took all this effusive service as his rightful due. "I will requite thee later, worthy host," he said grandly. "I will not fail to set thee before the king in the light of a trusty innkeeper." With this farewell he rode pompously out of the yard and slowly down the hill street to the river, and so passed out of the town. And, being out, he paused to consider his course.

"Shall I go to the fen in pursuit of them, or shall I go down Nottingham way?" he said. "I will go Nottingham way. I will be no more planted in mire like a rush. Nay, verily. Not to find all the young lords and Saxon serving-men in creation. I serve the king; and will go not into bogs and fens suitable for Saxon outcasts and no others. And if they be wise they will do the same."

Having come to this decision, he put spurs to Black Dick and was off southwest, while slowly Hugo and Humphrey journeyed on southeast. Presently the horse began to heave. "Why, where is thy speed of yesterday, Black Tom?" cried Walter Skinner. "Thou didst not heave when I clung round thy neck on the way to Lincoln town." He gave the bridle a sharp jerk, suddenly turning the horse which now began to show the spring-halt with which he was afflicted. "Why, what sort of a dance is this?" cried Walter Skinner.

"Thou art a strange beast. Verily, thou art like some people - one thing yesterday and another to-day. I can say this for thee - thou wert black yesterday, and thou art still black to-day."

He had not gone far when he came up with a man riding slowly along, and decided to take him into his confidence so far as to ask if he had seen those he sought. Accordingly he crowded Black Dick close alongside of the stranger's horse, and, giving him a meaning glance, said, "Hast thou seen a young lord this morn?"

The stranger looked astonished, as well he might.

"Ay," said Walter Skinner, much gratified. "I said a young lord. Mayhap thou art not used to consort with such, but a young lord is not much more to me than his Saxon serving-man. And that remindeth me - hast seen the serving-man also?"

"Nay," answered the stranger, mildly. "I have seen neither."

"And that is strange, too," said Walter Skinner. "Why, bethink thee, man! Thou must have seen them. They did leave Lincoln but yester morn. And if they came not this way, which way did they go? Answer me truly, for I warn thee, I serve the king."

The stranger reaffirming that he had seen neither the young lord nor his serving-man, Walter Skinner was obliged to be content. "They be as slippery as eels," he cried. "And that remindeth me, I did eat eels for breakfast at the Swan this morn."

Then, without a word of leave-taking, he rode off, Black Dick doing his afflicted best, and Walter Skinner wondering how he could have been so mistaken in the animal. "The thief that stole him did well to be rid of him," he said. "And that he should put him off on me is but another indignity I have suffered on this chase. The king hath ever a lengthening score to pay, and nothing but a dukedom will content me. And why should I not be a duke? Let Richard Wood say what he likes, worse men than I have been dukes. Ay, and more basely born."

By noon he had come to Newark. "And here will I pause and search the town for them," he said. "If they know not of them, why, their ignorance is criminal. A loyal subject should know what concerneth his king. And it concerneth the king that these two be found."

Now it chanced that the king was then at Newark and about to set off for Clipstone Palace. Which, when Walter Skinner heard, he declared proudly, "I will have speech of him."

"Thou have speech of him!" exclaimed an attendant. "Thou art mad."

"Nay, verily, I am not mad. Am I not Walter Skinner, hired by the king's minister to bide in a high tree that overlooketh De Aldithely castle? I tell thee, I will see the king." And, the party now approaching, he broke through all restraint and rode close up beside the king. "May it please thy Majesty," he began, "there be those that do keep me back from speech with thee. Ay, even though I do tell them that I serve thee."

The king looked at him, laughed rudely, and motioned

one of his attendants to remove him. But the little man waved the attendant off, and cried out so that all might hear, "Didst not thy minister hire me to bide in the tall tree that overlooketh De Aldithely Castle?"

At the mention of the name De Aldithely the king paused, and seemed to listen. Seeing which, Walter Skinner went on: "And, when all the rest were gone to York, did I not see the young lord and his Saxon serving-man ride forth? And did I not give chase? And do I not now seek them on this wind-broken and spring-halt horse as best I may?"

The king beckoned the little man nearer.

"Where hast thou sought?" he asked.

"In the wood, in the swamp, and in the town," was the proud answer. "I be not like Richard Wood, who did set out to help me. For I have come up with them three several times, and he not once."

The king turned to one of his attendants. "Take thou the madman into custody," he said. "We will presently send to De Aldithely castle to see if these things be so."

CHAPTER XV

Richard Wood and his men had searched the forest of Sherwood thoroughly enough to lead them to conclude that those they sought had taken another route. And on this, the tenth day of his chase, Richard Wood said decidedly: "We try the fen now to the east. They be not spirits to vanish in the air. Here in this wood they are not, nor do I think they would bide in any town. Therefore in the fen they must be." Thereupon, leaving the forest, they rode southeast by the way of Grantham, and so on into the fen country, striking it a few miles from where Hugo and Humphrey were making their camp for the night, almost within sight of Peterborough. The two were quite cheerful, and entirely unsuspicious that danger might be nearer to them than usual.

"Thinkest thou to stop at Peterborough?" asked Humphrey.

"Nay," replied Hugo; "there is no need."

"And yet," urged Humphrey, "a good lodging, were it but for one night, were a happy change from the fens. Who is the canon that is thine uncle's friend at Peterborough?"

"Canon Thurstan," replied Hugo.

"In the Canon Thurstan's house - " began Humphrey.

"But the canon hath no house," interrupted Hugo, with a smile.

"And how is that?" demanded Humphrey, with a puzzled air.

"It happeneth because this cathedral is on another foundation, and the canons here be regular and not secular, as they be in Lincoln."

Humphrey reflected. "I understand not," he said at length.

"At Peterborough the canons live all together in one house," explained Hugo. "Were we to go there we should be taken to the hospitium, where we should be lodged."

"And there see the Canon Thurstan?"

"Yea."

Again Humphrey reflected. Then he said: "The ways of priests be many. Mayhap I had known more of them, but in my forty years I have had to do with other matters, like serving my lord and lady in troublous times. The priest at the castle I did know, but not much of the ways of priests in priests' houses. And now cometh the evening mist right early. I will but make up the fire and then lead away the horses."

The fire made, although it was not dark, Humphrey departed, leaving Hugo to feed it. This the boy did generously, for he felt chilled. The smoke did not rise high and the odor of it penetrated to some distance.

In a little while Humphrey returned laden with a new supply of fuel partly green and partly dry. He then spread out their evening meal, and gave Fleetfoot his supper. And, all these things accomplished and the supper eaten, he announced his intention to go again for fuel.

"Have we not here enough?" asked Hugo. "Thou knowest we journey on in the morning."

"Mayhap," answered Humphrey. "I like not the look of this mist. My grandsire hath told me of a mist that lay like a winding-sheet on everything for two days, and this seemeth to me to be of that kind. It were not wise to stir, mayhap, to-morrow morn."

"Lest we encounter the other spy?" laughed Hugo.

"Jest not, dear lad," replied Humphrey, soberly. "We may not know how or whence danger cometh."

"And dost thou fear, then?" asked Hugo.

"Nay, I fear not. I cannot say I fear. But this moment a feeling hath come to me which I had not before. I will away for more fuel."

"I go with thee," said Hugo.

"Ay, lad, come," was the reply.

Two trips they made, each time returning heavily laden, and then Hugo laughingly said, "Surely we have enough, even if the mist last two days, for we had good store before thou didst look upon the mist with suspicion."

Humphrey smiled. "Yea, lad," he answered, "the fuel now seemeth enough."

While he spoke a wind sprang up and the mist grew lighter. It blew harder, and the mist was gone. One might see the stars. Two hours this lasted, during which Richard Wood and his men, as if guided, rode straight for the small camp, picking their way with great good fortune and making few missteps. Then the wind died down, the mist came back enfolding everything, and the pursuers encamped where they were. But of that Hugo and Humphrey knew nothing.

It might have been two o'clock when the serving-man awoke with a shiver and rose to renew the fire. He found it quite extinguished. As he felt about in the darkness for his flint and steel he glanced anxiously toward Hugo, though he could not see him. "I know not," he muttered, "I know not. But I did dream of eagles and they did scream above our heads. Some danger draweth near, or some heavy trouble."

The fire now blazed, and the faithful serving-man saw that Hugo was still asleep, resting as easily on his couch of reeds as he could have done on the canon's bed. "It is a good lad," said Humphrey. "Were he a De Aldithely he could not be better."

Humphrey lay down no more that night. Restlessly he moved about, now replenishing the fire, and now listening for some hostile sound. But he heard nothing.

It was late in the morning when Hugo awoke. "Surely

this must be thy grandsire's mist, Humphrey," he said. "It is heavy enough."

"Yea," answered Humphrey, looking up from the breakfast he was preparing. "It were best not to stir abroad to-day."

And at that moment Richard Wood was saying: "I smell smoke within half a mile of me. Ride we to see what that meaneth." Again, as if to aid him, the wind sprang up so that through the lifting mist one might easily pick his way, and Humphrey had just departed to look after the horses when Richard Wood and his men-at-arms arrived at the camp.

"Yield thee, Josceline De Aldithely!" commanded Richard Wood. "Yield thee in the king's name!" and, dismounting, he laid his hand on the astonished lad's arm.

A little later Humphrey, returning to the camp, paused in amazement, for he heard voices. He crept around a fringe of reeds and peered, but could not see clearly. He advanced further, still under cover, and then he saw.

"I did dream of eagles," he muttered, "and they did scream above our heads."

He listened, and from what he heard he learned that Hugo had not revealed himself as Hugo, but that he allowed the spy to think him to be Josceline. "Well did my lady trust in him!" exulted Humphrey. "And my lord shall know of this when we be come to France, as we shall come, though all the eagles in the fens do scream above our heads. And now I will away to the

Canon Thurstan, and see of what avail is the fish on the circlet of gold."

Creeping back as silently as he could, he mounted his horse and set out for Peterborough. "May the spy and his men-at-arms be too weary to stir till I come back," he said. "And if they be not weary, may the mist come lower down and hold them. And now, horse, do thy best. Splash into pools, wade, swim, do all but stick fast till we come to Peterborough town."

The horse, thus urged, did his sagacious best, and very shortly the serving-man was knocking at the gate of the porter's lodge. Now Humphrey knew nothing of how he ought to proceed. He only knew that he was in haste and that his need was urgent. He therefore determined to employ boldness and assurance, and push his way into the canon's presence.

"Canon Thurstan!" he cried boldly, attempting to push past the porter. "Canon Thurstan, and at once! My lord demandeth it."

"Thou mayest not push in past me thus," said the porter, stopping him. "Hast thou no token to show?"

"Yea, verily," answered Humphrey, hastily taking out his pouch and producing the prior's ring. "Take this, and bid the canon see me instantly."

The porter, calling an attendant, sent the ring by him. And presently an order came bidding Humphrey come into the presence of the canon.

"Where is the prior's nephew?" asked the canon, with the ring in his hand.

"In the custody of knaves who did surprise our camp."

"Knaves, sayest thou?" said the canon. "Wherefore hast thou a camp? Wherefore lodgest thou not in towns? What doest thou wandering through the fens?"

"We be pursued," answered Humphrey.

"Pursued? and by whom? Why, who should pursue the nephew of Roger Aungerville?"

"It is a king's man, and he hath with him three men-at-arms," answered Humphrey.

"A king's man, sayest thou? Nay, then, I meddle not in the king's matters." And he made as if to hand back the ring.

"And wilt thou not, then, aid me to rescue my young master?"

"Nay," answered the canon. "I may not do such a thing except upon compulsion. The dean is now absent, and I am in his place."

Beside himself with impatience over what seemed to him needless delay, and with disappointment over what seemed to promise failure altogether, Humphrey cried out roughly: "Compulsion, sayest thou? Then, since 'tis compulsion thou lackest, compulsion thou shalt have." And he laid hands on him.

At this two servants came running in. "Ye see," said the canon, turning to them. "This is the ring of my friend, Roger Aungerville, prior of St. Wilfrid's. It bindeth me to do all in reason for his nephew. This is his nephew's servant, who hath come to me to seek my aid to rescue his young master from the clutches of a king's man and three men-at-arms. I tell him I may not do such a thing except upon compulsion, and he layeth hands upon me." And he smiled upon them whimsically.

They understood the canon and his smile, and the first said: "If thou be compelled to aid this fellow, were it not best that I call up Herebald and Bernulf also? They be two, as thou knowest, swift of foot, and long of wind, and strong of arm; and they have two good staves, moreover."

"Why," said the canon, whimsically, "it were doubtless wholly evil that I should undergo compulsion in mine own domain by a strange serving-man, and be compelled to render aid even against the king's men. Still, since I be compelled to render aid, it were good to render the best possible, and so take with ye Herebald and Bernulf; and spare not for blows, so that ye bring off the young man safe."

Then he handed the prior's ring to Humphrey, who returned it to its pouch with great satisfaction. "I will ne'er say aught against a fish," he thought, "when it surmounteth a circlet of gold and doth belong to a prior. Methinks this canon liketh not the king nor his men, or he would not be so easily compelled to go against them, and so all shall yet be well with us."

The two servants now withdrew from the canon's presence, taking Humphrey with them, and, calling up Herebald and Bernulf, all four made speed to depart with the impatient serving-man.

"If the mist hold, we have them," said the first servant, as he rode beside Humphrey. "And it be heavier now than it was two hours agone."

"Ay, if we lose not our way," was the response.

"That we cannot do with Herebald and Bernulf," was the confident answer. "They were born and bred in these fens. And because they do hate the king and all his men they will be swift on the track this morn. If the king's man come not off with a broken pate, it will be a wonder. And the same is like to be the fate of the three men-at-arms."

The mist held, and, gleaming through it, as they neared the camp, they saw the red fire. Cautiously they approached. Richard Wood and his hungry men-at-arms had been making free with the packs so liberally provided by Humphrey at Lincoln, and were now resting on the rushes, with Hugo in their midst. They were in no mood to journey farther in the dimness of the mist, and Richard Wood was putting question after question to Hugo in the hope of eliciting some information which might be valuable to him, while the men-at-arms listened. They were Le Falconer's men, and they cared nothing for the fate of De Aldithely's son.

"Where hideth away thy mother?" asked Richard Wood.

"Even in the tomb," answered Hugo, truthfully, for his mother was dead.

For a moment Richard Wood was taken aback. "I had not heard of it," he said at length. "I knew not that thy mother was dead. The king had hoped to capture her also. But it seemeth death hath been beforehand with him."

And then the four servants of the canon, who had surrounded the little group unseen, lifted their staves and struck as one man. Over rolled Richard Wood and his three men-at-arms, stunned and unconscious. Humphrey at once brought up Hugo's horse and Fleetfoot, and the rescuers departed, leaving the four unconscious men to come to themselves at their leisure.

"Thou art to return to the hospitium," said the first servant to Humphrey. "It is the canon's order. He will see this nephew of the prior's and inquire more narrowly concerning his journey. And say thou naught of this rescue to any man. We four do the canon's bidding at all times, but our tongues wag not of the matter."

"When the canon is compelled, thou doest his bidding?" asked Humphrey.

"Ay, when he is compelled. He hath those of his kin who have suffered wrong at the king's hands. Therefore is he often compelled, as thou sayest, but he sayeth naught, and so the king knoweth naught. May he be long ignorant."

The first servant now withdrew himself from Humphrey's side, and in due time, still under cover of the friendly mist which spread its curtain over the streets of the town, the little party regained the hospitium unseen. As soon as their arrival was known Hugo was summoned to the presence of the canon; and the handsome, fearless youth, as he entered the room where the canon awaited him, seemed to strike his host with surprise.

"Thou the nephew of Roger Aungerville!" he exclaimed, when they were alone. "Thou shouldst be a De Aldithely."

"I am Hugo Aungerville," answered the boy. And then, drawing nearer, he half whispered something further to the canon, who seemed to find the explanation satisfactory.

"Why dost thou skulk and hide in this manner through the fens?" asked the canon. "And why art thou pursued?"

"I personate Josceline, son of Lord De Aldithely, and so draw pursuit from him. When I am come to Lord De Aldithely in France, then I shall make myself known, if need be."

"There will be no need," said the canon, decidedly. "And now, though I am glad to have succored the nephew of my friend, the prior, I am twice glad to do a service to Lord De Aldithely. Thou hast my blessing. Go now to thy rest, even though it be day. To-morrow morn I will send thee forth, if it seem best."

CHAPTER XVI

The king and his party rode on to Clipstone Palace. The attendant to whom the spy had been consigned hastily summoned a bailiff, to whom he made over his charge, and then galloped off to overtake the party. And Walter Skinner, hardly understanding what had come to pass, was left behind in Newark.

The king had thought to spend a week of pleasure at Clipstone, but the intelligence brought by the spy changed his plans. Of all his barons he hated Lord De Aldithely most. He would have struck at him more quickly and forcibly but for Lord De Aldithely's great popularity, and his own somewhat cowardly fear. And now here was the son escaped. And suddenly the evil temper of the king blazed forth so that his attendants, in so far as they dared, shrank from him.

The king waited not to reach Clipstone, but turning to two of his attendants he said: "Go thou, De Skirlaw, and thou, De Kellaw, to De Aldithely Castle. Put spurs to your horses and tarry not. See what is come to pass and bring me word again."

De Skirlaw and De Kellaw galloped off; and the king, shortly after coming to Clipstone, entered his private apartments and excluded the party from them.

"There is treachery somewhere," he said to himself, aloud, "and the guilty shall not escape me. Why, what is this Josceline but a boy of fourteen? And what is his mother but a woman? And do they both bid successful defiance to me, the king? I will have their castle down over their heads, and no counsels shall longer prevent me from doing it. Without the boy and his mother the father is sure aid to Louis. And where De Aldithely goeth, there goeth victory."

"Nay, not alway, my liege," responded a voice.

The king started, and turned to see one of his courtiers, more bold than the rest, who had quietly entered the chamber.

"I knew not of thy presence, De Kirkham," he said. "What sayest thou?"

"I say that victory is not alway with De Aldithely since he is a fugitive and his son a wanderer, and his castle in thy power."

"True. Thou sayest true," responded the king, after a pause. "Thou dost ever bolster up my failing courage. And I will have this silly boy, if the madman I did put in custody spake true. Yea, I will have him, though I set half England on the chase. His father is my enemy. And shall the son defy me? I will hale him to a dungeon, and so I tell thee, De Kirkham."

It was not a long ride to De Aldithely castle for those who need neither skulk nor hide, and the messengers of the king were at Selby ere nightfall. Here they determined to rest and go on the next morning. They heard no news in the town; nor did they see anything until they came to the castle itself. Birds of prey were screaming above the moat near the postern, and there was a stillness about the place that would have argued desertion if the flag had not still floated from one of the towers.

"I like not this stillness," said De Skirlaw.

"It hath a menacing air," observed De Kellaw.

A while the two waited in the outskirts of the wood near the cleared place about the castle. Then said De Skirlaw, "I go forward boldly to the bridge and summon the warder in the king's name."

"I go with thee," agreed De Kellaw.

So briskly the two rode forth from the shelter of the wood and up to the entrance, where De Skirlaw loudly wound his horn. But there was no response. He wound it again. And still there came no answer.

"Seest thou no man upon the walls?" asked De Skirlaw, scanning the heights with eyes somewhat near-sighted.

"I see no one," responded the hawk-eyed De Kellaw.

"Let us skirt the castle," proposed De Skirlaw, after a short pause.

"I am ready," responded De Kellaw.

Then together the two began their tour of examination. And the first thing they noted was the dam which William Lorimer and his men had constructed, and which the old warder had broken before he himself wandered forth from the castle, thus letting the water which had filled the rear part of the moat escape. From this point they rode back toward the entrance and, looking down into the moat, saw that it was dry. Turning again toward the postern, they noted the drawbridge there, and wondered to see it down. "The postern gate is also ajar," observed De Kellaw. The two now drew nearer and came even to the edge of the moat. They looked in, but saw only bones and armor; for kites and eagles had been at work, and nothing more remained of those who had perished there in the waters.

"Some strange thing hath happened here, and wind of it is not yet gone abroad," said De Skirlaw.

"Yea," agreed De Kellaw. "Darest thou venture across this bridge and in at the postern gate?"

"I dare," responded De Skirlaw. Dismounting, the two secured their horses by stakes driven into the earth, and then, on foot, crossed the bridge.

Inside the baileys all was deserted. The stables were empty. No footsteps but their own could be heard. No guard paced the walls. No warder kept watch. There was only silence and emptiness in the great hall, and no living creature was anywhere.

"Here be a mystery," said De Skirlaw. "I will not be the one to try to unravel it. Let us away to the king and say what we have seen."

"Ay, and brave his wrath by so doing," returned De Kellaw; "for, since he cannot lay hands on those that have disappointed him, he will lay hands on us that bring him word of the matter. To be near to the king, if thou be not a liar or a cajoler, is to stand in a dangerous place."

"Yea," answered De Skirlaw, "thou art right; but we needs must return. So let us set out."

While the king raged, Walter Skinner, left behind at Newark in charge of the bailiff, had speedily recovered his complacency.

"I have seen the king and spoken with him," he thought. "True, he did laugh right insultingly in my face, but that may be the way of kings; and even so will I laugh in the face of Richard Wood when next I see him, for he hath no hope of preferment and seeketh only his money reward. Therefore is he a base cur and fit only to be laughed to scorn."

When the scullions served him his dinner in the room where he was held prisoner, he looked upon them haughtily, and bade them mind what they did and how they did it. "For I shall not alway be served here by such as ye," he said.

"Nay, verily," replied the first scullion, "thou sayest true. Thou art more like to be served in one of the dungeons, if so be thou be served at all."

"Why, what meanest thou by that last, sirrah?" demanded the little man, strutting up and down and frowning.

"I did but mean that thou mayest shortly journey to that land where there is neither eating nor drinking," was the reply.

"Thou meanest that I may shortly die?" asked Walter Skinner, contemptuously.

"Yea," was the answer.

"Why, so must thou. So must Richard Wood. So must the king himself," said Walter Skinner. "But thou hast learned here so near the court to speak Norman fashion, and go round about the matter; and so thou speakest of journeys, and a land where there is neither eating nor drinking. Moreover, thou didst speak of dungeons. I would have thee know that they be no fit subjects of conversation in my presence. Have I not served the king? And shall I not therefore have preferment? Speak not of dungeons, and the country where there is neither eating nor drinking to me." And, seating himself, the pompous little man began to eat his dinner heartily. When he had finished, the first scullion came alone to take away the dishes.

"Thou art a very big little fool," he said, with a compassionate glance, "and so I bid thee prepare thyself for any fate. Thou must know that what thou saidst to the king did anger him. Thou didst bring him ill news, and the bearer of ill news he will punish."

Walter Skinner now showed some alarm; but he soon recovered himself. "Why, how now, sirrah?" he said. "I did not bid the young lord Josceline flee; but when he did flee I did give chase. And wherefore should I be punished for that? Had I remained in the tree near the castle, then indeed the king had had cause for anger."

The scullion still looked at him pityingly. "By thine

own showing," he said, "thou art but the king's spy, hired by Sir Thomas De Lany, no doubt. Spies have not preferment when their task is done, because, though the king doth take their work, he hateth them that perform it."

And now Walter Skinner stared in bewilderment. "Thou art but a scullion," he said at last. "And how knowest thou of Sir Thomas?"

"I am not what I seem," replied the scullion. "Wert thou sound in thy wits I would have said naught to thee, because then thou wouldst not have been here; but I like not to see one infirm of intellect run into calamity."

"And dost thou say of me that I be not sound in my wits?" demanded Walter Skinner, indignantly.

"Why, thou art either unsound of wit or a knave," was the calm response. "Only fool or knave doeth dirty work for another, even though that other be the king. And now, if thou wilt escape, I will help thee to it."

"I have had great toils," said Walter Skinner, with a manner which would have been ponderous in a man twice his size. "I have met a hedgehog. I have lost two horses. I have been planted in the mire like a rush. I have now come hither on a wind-broken and spring-halt horse, for which I did pay a price to a thief. And now thou sayest that for all this which I have undergone in the service of the king I shall have not preferment but a dungeon or death."

"Yea," was the calm rejoinder, "I say it; for where is the young lord? Knowest thou?"

"Nay," answered Walter Skinner, slowly.

"That is all that the king careth for of thee. That thou hast let him escape thee is all that he will note. And thy life will, mayhap, answer for it. All will depend on the greatness of his rage."

The little man looked in fright at the scullion, whom even his inexperienced eyes could now see was no scullion as he stood there in dignity awaiting the decision of the prisoner. "I will go with thee," he said, in a tremble. "But do I go on the wind-broken and spring-halt Black Tom of Lincoln?"

"That, Black Tom of Lincoln!" cried the mysterious scullion, laughing. "Thou hast once more been made a fool of. I have many times seen Black Tom. But thou shalt not go on the beast thou camest on. I will furnish thee another, for it must seem that thou didst escape on foot. Seek no more for the young lord. Flee into hiding and remain there. Dost thou promise me so to do?"

"Yea," was the prompt answer. "I promise."

He in the disguise of the scullion smiled, and bidding Walter Skinner follow him, led the way by secret passages until they came out unseen into a small court, where stood a horse ready saddled and bridled. The little man's guide bade him mount, and, opening a small door in the wall, motioned him to ride through it and away.

"My liege, the king," he said, as he watched the spy making all speed on his way, "thou wilt learn nothing of the flight of Josceline De Aldithely from thy late prisoner. And may confusion wait on all thy plans."

Walter Skinner had been gone over night, and the second day of his flight was well begun when the king, impatient over the slowness of De Skirlaw and De Kellaw, sent from Clipstone to Newark to have the spy brought before him. In haste the bailiff went to the room where he had placed him, and no prisoner was there. No prisoner was anywhere in the castle or in the town, as the frightened officer discovered after a diligent search. Only the afflicted horse upon which he had arrived remained in one of the stables. And with this word the unfortunate officer hastened on his way to the king. Near the gate, as he went out of Newark, he met one of the courtiers who bore a strong resemblance to him who had, in the guise of a scullion, set Walter Skinner at liberty. "Thou art frightened, worthy bailiff," he said. "But do thou only put a brave front on it and all may yet go well. Be careful to say and ever repeat that the man was mad, and not only mad, but cunning, and so hath made off, leaving his horse behind him."

The bailiff responded with a grateful look. "Thou art ever kind, my lord," he said. "And mayhap the man is dead. If he knew not the way, he may be dead, or caught by robbers. I will say that he may be dead also, and I hope he may be."

CHAPTER XVII

On the morning when Hugo and Humphrey were to start, the canon summoned them to his presence, and his face was grave. "I have but now learned," he said, "that the king is at Clipstone Palace. When the knaves thou didst leave stunned in the fen discover it also, they will at once repair thither, and that maketh a new complication of troubles. Let us consult together. I include the serving-man because he is such a valiant compeller." And the canon, forgetting his gravity, laughed heartily. And again he laughed. Then he grew grave again. "Pardon me," he said to Hugo; "but one may laugh so seldom in these troublous times. And erstwhile I was fond of laughing, and glad to have a merry heart. Now merry hearts be few in England, for they who have not already grief, have anxiety and dread for their portion." He paused and then went on: "The same hand that did send me news of the king's neighborhood did add something more thereto. A fierce little swaggering, strutting man did come upon the king at Newark and did tell him that Josceline, meaning thee, had fled, and that he had been pursuing thee. Didst thou know of it?"

"Yea," replied Hugo, with a smile. Then turning to the serving-man he said, "Humphrey, since the canon loveth to be merry, tell thou him of the hedgehog and the Isle of Axholme."

Humphrey did as he was requested, and was amply rewarded by the appreciation of his listener. "I see thou art worth a troop, my good Humphrey," he said, when the serving-man had finished. "Lady De Aldithely did well to trust thee with this lad. But now to my news once more. The king, in his wrath, will scour the country roundabout, and thou mayest not escape from him as thou didst from thine other pursuers. What dost thou elect to do?" And he looked at Hugo.

Hugo considered, and as he considered he grew pale. "I know not," he said at last. "It seemeth not safe to move."

"True," returned the canon. "Nor is it safe to remain here. The king respecteth no religious foundation. And when these stunned knaves in the fen make report to him, it will be known that thou wert seen close to Peterborough, and not an inch of the town will be left unsearched. I would my friend at Newark - but nay, I must not speak of that."

There was a brief silence, and Humphrey's was the most anxious face in the room. Not for himself did he feel anxiety, but for Hugo. If the canon hardly knew what to do, how could he hope to succeed in protecting the lad?

The canon was the first to speak. "If it can be done," he said, "the knaves in the fen must be kept from the king. I will have in to our conference Herebald and Bernulf." And rising, he summoned them.

They came in very promptly, and stood with cheerful faces before their master. "I know thee, Herebald; I know thee, Bernulf," said the canon, shaking his head at them in pretended reproof. "Ye be sad knaves both. What! would ye leave the monastery and go forth into the fen on ponies and armed with your staves? And would ye seek out once more the knaves ye did stun, and try to lead them astray, even down into the Broads? And all to keep them from the king?"

The two servants grinned.

"And would ye make believe to be on the trail of Hugo and Humphrey here? And would ye lead them far from the trail? I see that ye would, knaves that ye are. I have discovered ye. And there is no restraining ye when once ye have set your minds upon a thing. Therefore get ye gone to the fen. No man can say that I did send ye thither. And here be coins for ye both, which, no doubt, ye will deserve later, if not now."

The two joyfully withdrew and shortly afterward were in the streets of the town jogging slowly along as if bent on a most unwelcome journey. "See the Saxon sluggards!" commented a bystander. "Naught do they do but eat, unless compelled."

But once outside the town, the ponies were put to a good pace as the two hastened eagerly into the fen to trace, if they might, Richard Wood and his men-at-arms. The camp where they had come up with them before was deserted, and Herebald and Bernulf now had for their task the discovery of the direction the party had taken. Had they not been fen-men they might not have succeeded. But by night they felt that they were really on their trail. They had passed Peter-borough and continued on to the south, evidently going slowly, as became broken heads; and Herebald and Bernulf came up with them by the side of Whittlesea

Mere early on the following day. As they came into view Richard Wood evidently regarded the two Saxons with suspicion; but the men-at-arms looked at them with nothing but indifference.

Herebald and Bernulf appeared not to notice; but, withdrawing to a little distance, seemed to confer together and examine narrowly the leaves and twigs and rushes to see if they were bent or broken by the passage of a recent traveller. As they went earnestly about on all sides of the camp at the Mere, and keeping ever in sight of it, the curiosity of Richard Wood overcame his suspicion, and he beckoned them to approach. His summons they at first seemed inclined to disregard, but, as he continued beckoning, they at last went toward him with apparent reluctance.

"What seek ye?" demanded Richard Wood.

The two Saxons kept silence, but exchanged a crafty look, as if to say that they were not to be caught so easily.

"What seek ye?" repeated the spy.

"Hast thou seen aught of two runaways?" asked Herebald, gruffly. "Even a young lord who hath to his serving-man a Saxon?"

Then Richard Wood himself looked crafty. He did not like finding other pursuers so near him who might claim part of the reward, at least, when the search was successfully ended. But reflection came to his aid and told him that these Saxons were ignorant hinds who might be made useful on the search, and afterward cheated of their share of the reward. So he said, "Ye be fen-men, I know, or ye would not look so narrowly for a trail nor would ye find it. Which way do ye go?" And he looked at them keenly.

"Through the Broads toward Yarmouth," answered Herebald, slowly, after a short pause, and speaking in a surly tone.

"And wherefore?" demanded Richard Wood.

"There is shipping to be got to France from thence, is there not?"

"Yea, verily," cried Richard Wood. "It had not before entered my mind. Thinkest thou they have gone thither?"

Herebald frowned. "Thou art too ready with thy questions," he growled. "But this I will say, we go thither."

"Then we go with thee," said Richard Wood, firmly. "The way is open to us as well as to thee, and thou mayest not gainsay it."

"Oh, ay," returned Herebald, indifferently.

All that day Richard Wood kept a sharp eye on his new acquaintances. "Watch them narrowly," he said to his men. "They will seek to make this catch without us and so obtain the reward. Therefore all that ye see them do, do ye likewise, and I will also do the same."

Herebald and Bernulf saw and understood, and laughed together unseen. "They have not good wit, or they would not be so led by us when we be strangers," observed Herebald.

"It is ever thus with knaves," said Bernulf. "Though they seem sharp, there is a place where they be dull, and an honest man can often find it, and so outwit them."

Then they turned back to Richard Wood and his companions. "Go ye slowly and softly," growled Herebald. "Ye go lunging and splashing so that ye may be heard a long way off. Moreover, ye have scared up all the water-fowl hereabouts, and they go screaming over our heads. What think ye? If there be travellers near will they not hide close in the reeds till ye and your noise be past?"

At this rebuke Richard Wood drew rein suddenly and gazed sharply about him on all sides. Then he said, "Your caution shall be obeyed." And he gave the command to his followers to be careful.

Herebald now returned to the side of Bernulf, and the two, gazing with mirthful eyes into each other's faces, separated themselves a little distance and pretended to examine the way narrowly. It was not for nothing that they had served the merry Canon Thurstan for seven years.

That night, when all the camp was still, Bernulf slipped quietly forth in the darkness. He was gone three hours, and in that time he blazed such a trail as a madman might have taken. A bit of every fringe of rush or reed he came to he broke; and he stamped with his foot in the slimy mud on the edges of ponds and pools. "These fools," said he, "know naught of the fens or the Broads, and they will believe all that they see; for the broken bits and the footprints will speak to them of the young lord and his serving-man, and they will listen and hasten on. It is easy to lead a fool a chase."

The next morning Richard Wood was early awake, and, while all the rest were apparently asleep, he, in his turn, stole forth to look about him. "I trust not these knave Saxons entirely," he said to himself. "Though we all ride together now, they will seek to outwit us at the end, and gain the reward for themselves."

He had not gone far when he came upon the evidences of a recent passage along that way, and, in great excitement, he returned to the camp and roused up his followers, and, incidentally, the two Saxons. "Lie not here sleeping," he said, "when we be close on the trail. Let us be off speedily!" His men rose eagerly, and the Saxons also seemed to be stirred up at his words. And very soon, after half a breakfast, they all mounted and rode off, Richard Wood keeping in the advance. Soon he struck the trail blazed the night before by Bernulf, and eagerly he followed it, though he was obliged to do so slowly; for the trail went on ahead for three miles, then doubled, then zigzagged, then went straight east three miles, and bent round till it went due west again.

"The young lord is lost," declared Richard Wood, positively, "else would he never ride such a crazy track as this."

At last, when it was too late to travel further that day, the track turned eastward again, and the party went into camp for the night about one mile from where they had camped the night before. But to Richard Wood it seemed that they must be at least ten miles advanced on their way, for, to him, all the marsh looked the same.

"Did I not do well, Herebald?" asked Bernulf. "Here have we kept them busy in the marsh for a whole day, and that giveth the lad with the canon so much the better a start."

"Yea," said Herebald. "To-night rest thou, and I will start the trail for them to-morrow."

Accordingly, as soon as the weary Richard Wood and his men had sunk into a heavy sleep, which they did almost as soon as they lay down, Herebald set out. He was extremely swift of foot and knew the region well. He was gone four hours. "The knave king's man and his followers will sleep soundly to-morrow night also if they follow my trail," he said, when he had returned and lay down.

The next morning a late awakening of the men gave a late start. The enthusiasm of the day before was gone; but it came back when Richard Wood, riding in advance, struck the trail once more. This was more difficult to follow than the one of the day before. It led through places where the party almost mired, but not quite; through places where the horses splashed heavily along, scaring the water-fowl up in all directions; through patches of reeds; through tangles of tough grass; through shallow water; through deep water; and ever on with few seeming deviations. But the course was much slower than that of the day before, and that had been slow enough.

Night came and the fagged party in disappointment once more lay down.

"Thou hast done well, Herebald," said Bernulf. "To-night it is my turn. But think ye not it were better now to lead straight on to Yarmouth?"

"Yea," answered Herebald.

"It seemeth to me that it were best to put them there to search the town. What thinkest thou?"

"Even as thou thinkest," returned Herebald, grinning.

"And then," continued Bernulf, "methinks it would be seemly to entice them aboard a fishing-vessel and ship them off for France, and so be rid of them."

"Yea," agreed Herebald. "I would all the knaves in England were shipped off to France, and it were a good beginning to ship these four."

Another morning dawned, and slowly and heavily the men arose. Such weary days followed by nights spent in the marsh had sapped their energy. For the first time the men-at-arms looked sullen, and one went to Richard Wood and spoke for all. "We be neither fish nor water-fowl," he said, "to spend our days in the marsh. We go this one day more with thee; then, if we come not out of the marsh and into the town of Yarmouth, we leave thee and return to our master."

The heavy-eyed Richard Wood counselled patience. "Would ye have these Saxon knaves get the better of us just when the quarry is all but run to earth? They be not so weary as we, and a plague upon their endurance. If ye stand not by me, the game is lost."

But the man-at-arms answered sullenly: "I have said. Lead us out of this vile marsh."

CHAPTER XVIII

"And now," said the canon, when Herebald and Bernulf had gone, "thou mayest remain no longer here. It is too near the king, and moreover, delay taketh thee not forward toward France. Since thou knowest not what to do, Hugo, I will plan for thee. And first, thou must leave here with me thy dog, Fleetfoot."

Hugo opened his mouth to object, seeing which the canon at once continued, "Nay, do not speak. It must be done. Thee I can disguise and thy man Humphrey I can disguise, but what disguise availeth for thy dog? To take Fleetfoot is to endanger thy life unnecessarily. Shouldst thou take him, even if thou didst win safely through, which is a very doubtful thing, thou wouldst find him but an unwelcome encumbrance to Lord De Aldithely. Leave the dog, therefore, with me, and I will care for him."

Hugo reflected. Then he looked up into the canon's face, and he saw that, though he might have a merry heart, he had also a determined will. He yielded, therefore, and consented to leave Fleetfoot behind. At this decision the canon smiled well satisfied, and Humphrey's face also showed the relief he felt at being rid of the dog's company.

"And next," continued the canon, "I counsel thee to go

no more through the fens, for there will they seek for thee. Thou hast gone skulking and hiding so far on thy course, and they that pursue thee will be too dull to think that thou mayest change. The time is come for thee to proceed boldly and on the highway. I will send thee first to Oundle, which lieth southwest from hence, and with a token I will procure thee safe lodging there. From thence I can do no more for thee till thou come to St. Albans, twenty miles away from London. But from Oundle thou must take thy course still southwest till thou come to the Watling Street. Then follow that southeast down to St. Albans. And in this jaunt Humphrey must lead, and thou must follow; for I shall make of Humphrey a priest, and of thee a novice."

He ceased, and there was no reply to what he had said. Both Hugo and Humphrey would have preferred to ride clad as they were, and to choose their own route and stopping-places. But they were sensible of how much they already owed the canon, and dangers were now so thick about them that they feared to refuse to do as he bade them. Therefore they permitted themselves to be properly robed, and took meekly the instructions he gave them as to their speech and manner of behaviour.

"This I do not for thee only, but for my friend, Roger Aungerville, and for the brave Lord De Aldithely," he said in parting from them. "Forget not to call me to their minds when thou dost meet them, and say that I be ever ready to serve them as best I may."

Hugo promised, and thanked the canon on the part of himself and Humphrey for the cheer and aid they had received at his hands; and, with a heavy heart, rode away behind the serving-man, who was now turned into a priest. He thought not on the dangers of the way, but on Fleetfoot, left at Peterborough.

"Fret not, dear lad," said Humphrey. "In the king's dungeon there would be no room for Fleetfoot, and mayhap he would be put to death. Now is he in good hands, even in the merry-hearted canon's hands, and no evil will befall him. He hath such a care to please thine uncle and my lord that he will look well to thy dog."

By nightfall the two were safely lodged at Oundle.

"Ye be safe," said the priest of the parish when he had received them. "Here will no man seek for ye this night, and, on the morrow, ye shall speed away. I may not suffer ye to tarry longer."

Meanwhile the unlucky bailiff had proceeded to Clipstone with the news that Walter Skinner was fled, and no man knew what had become of him. He had just delivered it and the king was still in his rage when De Skirlaw and De Kellaw arrived. "Admit them," he gave order. "I will hear what hath come to pass there. Mayhap the castle hath stolen away, even as this prisoner hath done."

As De Skirlaw and De Kellaw entered, the king, scanning their faces, read that they bore him no welcome news, and his rage broke out afresh. "What land is this that I be king of?" he exclaimed. "A land of rebels and disobedience. A land of dull skies and duller fortunes. What saw ye that ye come before me with glum faces and serious looks? Speak, if ye can. Is the castle gone?"

"Nay, Your Majesty," said De Skirlaw. "The castle we

found, but -"

"Ye mean that the prisoner spake true," burst out the king, "and that the young lord is escaped?"

"Yea," answered De Skirlaw. "No human being inhabiteth the castle. And in the moat at the rear kites and eagles have fed."

"What mean ye? What hath chanced there?"

"Your Majesty, no man knoweth," was the answer.

"But there be only bones and armor in the dry moat, and no living thing in the castle."

For a little the king stared straight before him. Then he said, "Bring the rascal bailiff before me."

With haste the unhappy officer was brought.

"Wretch!" broke out the king. "Go find me the prisoner that thou hast let escape thee. If thou find him not, thy life shall answer for it." In great fear the bailiff retired from the royal presence, and the king went on as if to himself: "Mayhap he knew what hath chanced. Mayhap he knoweth now the whereabouts of the young lord."

As the bailiff reentered Newark he met again the courtier by the gate. "What news, worthy bailiff?" he asked.

"Why, this," answered the bailiff, in despair. "The prisoner must be found or my life is forfeit. And I know not where to look."

The courtier kept silence for a few moments. "The prisoner must not be found," he thought, "or mayhap the young lord, Josceline De Aldithely, will be undone; and for the friendship I do bear his father, this may not be. But neither must the worthy bailiff die." Then he spoke.

"Worthy bailiff," he said, "what is done cannot be undone. The prisoner is gone, no man knoweth whither. Thy only hope is in flight. And to that, seeing thou art a worthy man, I will help thee. Go thou apparently to seek for the prisoner, but flee for thy life, and tell me not where. Thou knowest a place of safety, I warrant thee."

"Yea," replied the bailiff, after a little thought, "I know."

"Proceed, then, with thine helpers to the search for the prisoner; contrive shortly to give them the slip, and thou art saved. I will do what I can in baffling pursuit of thee. For this our king is, as thou knowest, a tyrant who, though he greatly feareth death for himself, doth not hesitate to measure it out to us his subjects. Therefore are we bound to help each other. When thou canst protect another, do so; and so farewell." Speaking in these general terms he not only gained from the bailiff a belief in his own benevolence, but effectually concealed from him the real reason of his helping him, which was to protect, so far as possible, the young Josceline De Aldithely.

"It is well for a lad when his father hath many friends," mused the courtier. "For then, even the malice and hatred of the king may be foiled. I will now away to Clipstone and see what passeth there. " And, summoning two attendants, he set out.

Upon arriving, he found but a gloomy air about the place. The king's rage was not yet spent and no man knew upon whom he would take occasion to visit his displeasure. But the courtier who, in the guise of a scullion, had himself set the prisoner free, moved calmly about, and alone of all seemed to feel no anxiety. Toward nightfall the word was whispered about that, on the morrow, the king would himself proceed with a party to De Aldithely castle.

The morrow came and at an early hour there was everywhere bustle and confusion, for all that the royal party would need for their brief absence from Clipstone must be taken with them: food, dishes, bedding, and servants.

At length all was ready and the train set out. It was a gloomy ride, for the king's temper was not yet recovered and no man ventured to say aught in his presence.

Leaving the baggage and servants far in the rear, the impatient king with his attendants rode on and on until they came to Cawood castle beyond Selby and but a few miles distant from De Aldithely castle. Here the king stopped for the night, and the servants and baggage not having yet come up, his temper was not improved by the lack of their service. It was a great castle to which he had come, being one of the largest and strongest in the north of England.

"And Cawood shall have no more for a neighbor the castle of De Aldithely," said the king the next morning, when, after a somewhat uncomfortable night owing to the late arrival of the servants, he rode forth from its gate on his way to the home of the great and popular baron.

Artisans from Selby who had been sent by the king's order, were already on their way thither also. And these having risen very early and made good speed, John found already arrived when he himself appeared. But no one had ventured to set foot within the walls without the royal word.

As John drew near, he looked upon the castle in scowling silence. Still in silence he rode to the edge of the moat and looked down. And there he saw the armor and the bones as De Skirlaw had said. An attendant now spoke to him, and he nodded his head in assent. At once three of the artisans were hurried across the postern bridge and through the gate with instructions to hasten to the front entrance and let down the bridge and open the great gate for the king.

Still speaking no word the monarch rode to the great gate, crossed the bridge, and entered, and once within the outer bailey, looked about him. He rode into the inner bailey, and, dismounting, began a personal examination of the castle; and as he proceeded his frown grew blacker and blacker, for everywhere he saw evidences of premeditated and deliberate flight. The treasure chests were empty, and everything of value removed.

At last he spoke. "What hath chanced here I know not," he said. "But this I know, these traitor walls shall stand no longer. Bid the artisans in to begin their destruction." Then turning to De Skirlaw he added: "Go thou to the moat and examine the armor. See, if

Gulielma Zollinger

thou canst, to what troop it belongeth."

But before De Skirlaw could execute this commission there appeared upon the scene two men-at-arms from Hubert le Falconer, in search of certain of their companions, and they were at once brought before the king. To him they related how, for a certain sum, a certain knight in the service of the king had hired them to assist him in entering the castle, through the treachery of one Robert Sadler, and in carrying off the young lord, Josceline De Aldithely, to the direct custody of the king.

"And this knight was - " interrupted John.

"Sir Thomas De Lany," said the man-at-arms.

"Came thy companions to the castle here?" demanded the king.

"Yea, Your Majesty, some ten days now agone. My master having need of them hath sent us to call them to him again."

"It is a call they will not answer," said John. "Nor will the brave knight, Sir Thomas De Lany, answer to my call. De Kirkham, take these men-at-arms to view the moat by the postern. Now know we who sleep there. Could we but know the whereabouts of the wife of this traitor, De Aldithely, and the whereabouts of his son, we were better satisfied. And now depart we from this place. Raze the walls. Let not one stone remain upon another.

"And thou, De Skirlaw, and thou, De Kellaw, haste ye both to Newark and see if the rascal bailiff hath yet found the prisoner. He can speak if he will, and he must be found."

With feigned zeal the two set out, but, once beyond the view of the king, their fiery pace lagged to a slow one as they rode toward Selby, where they were determined to halt for a night's rest. "I care not if the prisoner be not found," said De Kellaw. "I be tired of this tyranny; this imprisoning and slaying of children taken as hostages from their fathers; this razing of castles. John will not be king forever, and it behooveth us not to make ourselves odious to all men by helping him to his desires too much. I haste not on this enterprise, and so I tell thee."

"Nor I neither," declared De Skirlaw.

The king now set out on his return to Cawood, from whence, on the morrow, he would go on to Clipstone again.

"Yea, and I will go even to Newark," he said to himself as he rode along. "I will be at hand to put heart into this search, which seemeth to lag. But have the prisoner I will; and when I have found him, I will open his mouth for him to some purpose."

CHAPTER XIX

To the great joy of Richard Wood, the way seemed to lead across the wide, flat, marshy country straight in the direction of Yarmouth. "If the young lord and his serving-man be as weary of the marsh as I and my companions be," he said, "they have gone directly out of it to Yarmouth, and there shall we catch them."

But though the way seemed not to deviate in direction, that of the day before was easy in comparison with it.

"Were I but journeying through this vile stretch of country I could pick a better course," grumbled Richard Wood as he went forward. "But being on chase of these two, I must even be content to follow. Behold me now when the day is but half gone, slopped with water and besplashed with mud till no man may know the color of my garments. It must be that the young lord hath small wit to take such a course. Or mayhap he looketh more behind him than before as he rideth, fearing pursuit."

And now they were come to the Yare; and it seemed that they would be obliged to swim across it. "Never swam I in my life," declared Richard Wood, "and I will not now begin."

"Canst thou not swim on thy horse's back?" demanded

one of the men-at-arms, impatiently.

"Ay; but how if the beast goeth down in the stream?" said Richard Wood. "I tell thee, I fear water."

Then came one of the Saxons to the rescue. "Near here dwelleth a fen-man," he said, "and he hath a boat. I will e'en call him to take thee over, and thou canst let thy horse swim."

Upon hearing this all three of the weary men-at-arms clamored for places in the boat which Herebald, after a conference with Bernulf, promised them.

"Hearest thou not, Herebald," said Bernulf, "that the king's man feareth the water? We must put him and his men across softly and bolster up their valor, else shall we fail to entice them aboard the fishing-vessel, and so fail to ship them off to France; and thus England is so much the worse off by having still here the vile knaves."

"Yea, Bernulf, thou art right," was the answer. "And surely we have led them through toils enough, for they be weary to fainting. This it is for a vile spy to go round the country with some lumbering men-at-arms, seeking to entrap a poor young lad to his destruction."

"Yea," replied Bernulf; "but thou hast left out one thing. Thou shouldst have said, 'This it is when two Saxons get him and them in the toils.' They had not been one-half so weary without us. Do but remember that."

"Ay," agreed Herebald. "I do think we have some blame for their aching bones; but they can rest when they be tossing on that good old North Sea, for I promise them it will take more than a load of herring to hold the ship steady."

All this time Richard Wood and his men were impatiently waiting. "Why tarry ye so long?" called the spy in a loud voice, as he looked in their direction.

"We did but talk of what 'twere best to do and a few other matters," replied Herebald, advancing. "And we think we may promise places to ye all in the boat. Run, Bernulf; make speed and bring the man and his boat."

Away went Bernulf, leaping lightly across a pool here, picking his way skilfully over long grass and among reeds there, to the amazement of Richard Wood, who watched. "I would my horse had but the nimbleness and speed of the knave's legs," he said. "But our toils be almost over, and so I complain not. I make no doubt we lay hold of the young lord and the serving-man in Yarmouth."

At this Herebald looked sceptical.

"What meanest thou by that look?" asked Richard Wood.

"Why, nothing," returned Herebald. "Only I did call to mind that there be many fishing-vessels in the harbor."

"And what hath that to do with it?" asked Richard Wood.

"And through the North Sea one may go to France."

"Why, thou didst say that long ago when we were

toiling through the marsh. Thinkest thou I shall forget to search the ships when I have searched the town? I forget not so easily, I promise thee."

The fen-man seemed not to be readily persuaded to bring his boat, for an hour elapsed before he was seen rowing toward them with Bernulf lolling lazily in the stern.

At last he reached the little party, and Richard Wood and his men were safely embarked. Then the two Saxons, mounting their ponies, directed them into the stream, and they were off, the fen-man glancing curiously every now and then at his passengers. He made no remarks, however, but managed his boat so skilfully that Richard Wood hardly realized that he was on the water, and, in due time, found himself set ashore with his men on the other side.

"And yonder be Yarmouth," said Herebald, cheerfully. "We come to it surely by set of sun."

There was no more marks of passage before them, and Richard Wood, picking his own path, travelled more easily than he had before, and had also to help him an enlarged appreciation of his own powers, to which he speedily added a large increase of hope that now the end of his troubles had come. He therefore went forward with renewed animation, and when, at set of sun, he stopped before a little Yarmouth inn, he was well satisfied with himself.

"Do ye also lodge here?" he asked the Saxons.

Herebald affected to be uncertain.

"Surely it were better that ye do so," urged Richard Wood, "that we may search the town and the ships together on the morrow."

"Nay," put in Bernulf. "We lodge not here. I do know a cheaper place; and we be not Normans that we have money to waste."

Richard Wood frowned. "Speak not against the Normans," he said. "The king is a Norman."

"Oh, ay," answered Bernulf, indifferently. And then he added with determination in his tone, "We lodge not here."

Herebald now drew Richard Wood aside.

"Heed him not," he said, "lest he turn surly on our hands and get us into trouble. I will go with him elsewhere to lodge, and to-morrow morn will I bring him back to help thee on thy search."

"Thou art not so sad a knave as he," returned Richard Wood, "and I thank thee. See that ye both come, and that right early."

Herebald reiterated his promise to do so, and then went away with Bernulf, while Richard Wood followed his men into the bar, where they were already drinking.

"What meanest thou, Bernulf? Why wouldst thou not lodge here?" asked Herebald as they rode along.

"Why, this, Herebald," was the answer. "We have much to do ere we go to rest. We must find the ship that is loaded and ready to weigh anchor to-morrow toward noon when the wind and tide will serve. And we must bespeak the help of the captain to get these knaves aboard."

"True, Bernulf," responded Herebald. "Thou hast a wit that would match with the canon's."

"Yea, I be not so dull as some Normans, though I be counted but a slow-witted Saxon," returned Bernulf, with complacency. "And now let us first to our supper and the putting away of the ponies, and then do we take boat and visit the ships."

They found an inn suited to their tastes in one of the Rows, and before the dark had really come down over the harbor they were out on a tour of the ships. The tour, however, was destined to be a short one, since the second ship they visited proved to have among her sailors two men that they knew. And, moreover, they discovered the captain to be one Eric, whose mother was cousin to Bernulf's father.

"Here have we luck," said Bernulf. "To Eric may I speak freely."

"Yea, verily," answered Herebald. "And she is loaded with herring also and saileth on the morrow toward noon. Go, then, and speak freely, as thou sayest."

Bernulf did so; and the Captain Eric entered heartily into his plans as Bernulf laid them before him. "The loons!" he exclaimed with a hearty laugh, as he heard of the journey through the fens. "The witless geese! And thou hast not once told them that the young lord and his serving-man came in this direction?"

"Nay, not once. We did but break branches, and make tracks on the edges of the pools, and ruffle the long grass, and they did read for themselves that those they sought were just ahead of them. We have hope that the young lord be, by this time, well and safely sped on his journey."

"Ay, and by to-morrow at this time will his pursuers be upon their journey," said Eric. "I am to refuse to let them come aboard, sayest thou, until they demand permission in the king's name? And then the moment they be down the companionway I am to hoist the anchor and be off?"

"Yea," answered Bernulf, "that is it."

"So be it," returned Eric. "And it is a small thing to do for a kinsman also moreover."

"And now go we ashore," said Bernulf. "To-morrow morn we aid the king's spy to search the town. He will have a merry run up and down the Rows, he and his men." And, with a hearty farewell to the skipper, Herebald and Bernulf climbed down the side of the vessel to their little boat gently rocking alongside.

"The business in hand hath an early end when luck goeth with a man," observed Bernulf, with satisfaction.

"Yea," responded Herebald. "And luck most often goeth with the man that hath good wit of his own."

Their strong arms made light of the short distance they had to row, and they were soon back at the little inn and at rest.

As for Richard Wood, weary as he was, he was long in finding sleep. For ever he would be wondering in which part of the little town it were best to begin the search. And how it were best to conduct it so that no outsider could manage to claim part of the reward when the runaways were captured. At last, undecided, he fell asleep, and Herebald and Bernulf were awaiting him when he awoke rather late in the morning. In haste he and his men ate their breakfast, and in still greater haste they set off on the search, only to be brought to a standstill before it was well begun; for there fronting the sea were one hundred and forty-five little narrow streets called the Rows, and their combined length made a distance of seven miles.

"This be a foolish way to build a town," grumbled Richard Wood, "and none but Saxons would have done it. Why, here be a street only two feet wide at one end of it. And up and down one hundred and forty-five streets we must chase, to say nothing of looking in the better parts of the town."

"Thou hast well said," observed Herebald, gravely. "It is not an easy thing, this search. But where dost thou begin? And how wilt thou go about it?"

"Why, why," stammered Richard Wood, "I did never search a town before, and that is but the truth."

"Were it not best to proceed boldly?" asked Herebald, slyly.

"Boldly, sayest thou? And what meanest thou by boldly?"

"Why, by boldly, I mean boldly. Surely thou knowest

what boldly is? Walk into the house with a 'by your leave,' which is, after all, no leave, since it is done without leave; there look through all, and then out and away again into the next house, or the next but one, as it pleaseth thee."

Richard Wood looked at him in displeasure. "It is easy to see thou art but a Saxon churl," he said. "And moreover, where is thy sense of time? This day were gone; ay, and the next before we had entered every house in one hundred and forty-five little streets."

"Ay, thou art right. Perchance it were better not to take so much time, for there be the ships, and some of them do sail to-day."

"To-day!" exclaimed Richard Wood, in alarm. "And when?"

"Toward noon," was the reply; "for then wind and tide will serve."

A look of resolution came over the face of Richard Wood. He turned to his men-at-arms.

"Take each of thee a street," he said, "and I will take another. Search as well and thoroughly as ye can for one hour, and then come to this point to go with me to the ships. We have had many toils to catch them. They must not escape us now."

"And what do we?" asked Herebald.

Now Richard Wood was quite determined that the Saxons should not share in the reward, so he answered: " Stand ye here , and watch all who pass. Let none escape ye."

"That were an easy task," growled Bernulf. "But why may we not also take each man his street, and knock and 'by-your-leave' with the rest of ye? It is because we be Saxons that ye put this slight upon us." And he affected to be greatly displeased.

"Peace, man!" said Richard Wood, more pacifically. "It is true ye be Saxons, but that is by the will of heaven. And ye be in nowise to blame therefor. So should ye bear with patience the lot of Saxons."

"Which is to wait on Normans, as ye would say," retorted Bernulf, scornfully. "But we bide here, as thou hast said."

"The hinds be jealous," said Richard Wood, as he hastened up the little street he had chosen, looking narrowly about him for the house, in his judgment, most likely to be the hiding-place of the runaways. About half-way up the street he espied it, but when, in the king's name, he entered, he found nothing to reward him for his pains. Wherever he stopped he fared no better, and he was fain to believe, at last, the asseverations of the inhabitants that there were not only no runaways in that street, but that none were to be found in all Yarmouth, - a town which, according to them, was a most proper place, where those who could not give a good account of themselves never ventured. Unless, indeed, it might be a few Frenchmen now and then, and, as they told him with much garrulity, every Englishman knew what to expect from the French. And then they asked him if those he sought were French. And when he said that they were not, they began at the beginning and went all over the subject again, telling him what a discreet and proper place Yarmouth was, and how none such as he was seeking ever ventured there, until he was like to go distracted, and had not completed the search of even that one little Row when the hour was up, and he hastened to the place appointed to meet his men-at-arms. He found that his experience had been theirs, and, in his disappointment and disgust, he said some harsh things about Yarmouth tongues, which he estimated as entirely too nimble.

The two Saxons heard his comments with covert smiles, and followed along toward the ships.

That morning the ship of Eric had slightly changed her position, and Bernulf so managed that, when the small row-boat he was bidden to hire was about to put off from land, Eric's ship would naturally be the first one boarded.

"Do we go with thee?" asked Herebald.

"Nay," answered Richard Wood. "Here be two men who will row for us. Do ye stay where ye be and watch."

Then they all climbed into the small row-boat and were pulled away toward Eric's ship.

"Ay, we will watch," said Herebald to Bernulf.

A little later the boat went alongside, and the spy and his men-at-arms climbed heavily and clumsily aboard, after a brief parley with skipper Eric, in which he had at first refused them permission to do so.

"They be here!" exulted Richard Wood in his thought,

"else why should we be forbidden to come aboard?"

"What seek ye?" demanded the skipper, in a gruff tone when they were safely on deck.

"Two runaways," answered Richard Wood, loudly, for already the anchor was being lifted.

"There be no runaways here," returned the skipper, positively.

"We will see, we will see," returned Richard Wood. And laying firm hold of the rail he lunged down the steep companionway, followed by his men-at-arms and one of the seamen, whom the captain by a nod of his head bade to follow them. Once down, they gazed about them and knew not which way to turn.

"Where is the captain?" said Richard Wood, sternly. "Bid him come down and show us all parts of the ship at once."

"Skipper may not come. He is busy," answered the seaman. "But I can show thee. Thou wilt see all?"

"Yea, all."

Then the seaman very obligingly began to do as he was bid. There was very little to see in the close quarters; but he, being loquacious, was a long time in showing it, and more than half an hour had elapsed before Richard Wood was thoroughly persuaded that there was nobody secreted on board. And all this time, in his eagerness, he had not noticed that the ship was moving. He now turned to the companionway.

"What motion is this?" he asked, turning pale. "Hath the ship gone adrift from her moorings?"

"Nay," answered the seaman; "the ship is not gone adrift."

Laying fast hold on the rail, the spy managed to climb up to the deck. He looked about him, but no row-boat was alongside. He then turned to the skipper.

"Surely we be gone adrift from our moorings," he said.

"Nay," answered the skipper, calmly. "I did forbid thee to come aboard, but thou wouldst come. Now are we under sail."

CHAPTER XX

The priest of the parish at Oundle had Hugo and Humphrey up and off betimes the next morning, as he had said. "It must be he liketh not our company over well," observed Humphrey, as they jogged on after a very brief and hasty leave-taking.

"Perhaps he taketh thee for a wolf in sheep's clothing," said Hugo, with a meaning glance at the priest's habit in which the stalwart Humphrey was engulfed.

"And thee for the cub, dear lad," retorted Humphrey. "But it may be after all that he looketh but to his own safety, and desireth not to fall into disgrace with the king by harboring us. But hark! Let us withdraw ourselves into the wood. Here come travellers this way. And I cannot feel safe in the priest's garb. The wood, methinks, were a better protection."

With the celerity of practice the two concealed themselves in the wood in such a position that they could see the path. And presently there came into view a small party of knights on their way northward.

"They look not so dangerous," commented Hugo.

"Nay," agreed Humphrey. "I would liefer see them than king's spies. But bide we here a bit and see if

Gulielma Zollinger

more will come."

It was very still in the wood that morning and a little sound seemed a great one. So the two, while they waited, talked together in low tones. "The merry-hearted canon is in most things wise, I do suppose," observed Humphrey. "But I feel not like a priest though I wear his garb. And I fear to do something which will betray me to be but the Saxon serving-man which I am. Still, I must wear it?" And he looked inquiringly at Hugo.

"Yea," replied the boy. "The land is so full of priests that few scan them closely. And, moreover, there be Saxons among them. He was born but a Saxon serf who was the great pope Adrian IV."

"Sayest thou so?" said Humphrey. "I will e'en take courage and wear the priest's garb as well as I can. I suppose thou knowest all this from thine uncle, the prior?"

"Yea," answered Hugo, with a smile.

A while there was silence, while both listened. Then Humphrey said, "But I like not the canon's plan that we go to St. Albans."

"And wherefore?" asked Hugo.

"That I cannot tell. I do but know that I like it not. It were better to go straight to London. So think I, and so do I say."

Hugo reflected. He knew that the way was not particularly safe for them anywhere. "If it should be discovered that we have been at Peterborough," he said at length.

"Yea, lad," broke in Humphrey. "I had not thought of that. But would they not straight seek for us at St. Albans, where the merry-hearted canon hath sent us? And neither did I like the parish priest at Oundle. He did speed us too gladly. And he knoweth that we go to St. Albans."

"Thou mayest be right, Humphrey," said Hugo. "It will doubtless cost the monks at St. Albans small grief if they do not see us. We will go to London as thou sayest."

Humphrey regarded him approvingly. "It is easy to see that thou art far from being a fool," he said. "Hiding and skulking through wood and fen are making thee wary."

The two now resumed their journey, and Humphrey asked, "Hast ever been on this Watling Street?"

"Nay," replied Hugo. "I was bred up, as thou knowest, by mine uncle, the prior, and all my travels have been by ear. What I did hear him speak of I know, but not much else."

"And he did never speak of the Watling Street?"

"Yea, he hath oft spoken of it. But it is a long road, and here in England since the time of the Romans. I know that it goeth to London."

"Then we go to St. Albans after all?"

"Why, St. Albans lieth on the Watling Street. So said the Canon Thurstan. But we need not stop long there."

"Unless we be stopped," said Humphrey. "I would we need not go nigh the place." He now halted and looked about him carefully. "Said the priest at Oundle where we should first come to the Watling Street?" he asked. "Nay," replied Hugo. "He did say only, 'Go till thou come to it,' even as the Canon Thurstan said."

"I hope we be on the right way," observed Humphrey. "I would fain find not only the Watling Street, but a town and an inn also. For the breakfast of the priest at Oundle was more of a fast than a feast."

They were now traversing an undulating country and going in a southerly direction.

"We may not ask our way," said Humphrey, decidedly. "It is as much as I can do to wear the priest's garb and speak when I be spoken to. Were I to speak of myself, it would speedily be known that I was no priest, for I have not the mind of a priest."

Hugo smiled. He had already learned that, although one might turn the mind of Humphrey for a little from its accustomed track, yet it speedily turned back. He had taken a little courage at the mention of the Saxon pope, Adrian IV, but now he was as fearful as ever.

"I wear this garb only till we be through London," resumed Humphrey. "The Canon Thurstan bid me wear it only so far. He said naught of what should be done later. And once we leave London I will be again Humphrey the serving-man, and no make-believe priest. I like not make-believes."

Hugo smiled again. "How likest thou my being a make-believe Josceline, and no Hugo?" he asked.

"That be a different matter," was the decided answer. "Thou hast saved our young lord's life, and thou art a brave lad. But I would rather skulk and hide in the fen than in the priest's garb. How likest thou to be a novice?"

"Why, very well," replied Hugo, "so that it serve my turn and help me on my way in safety. I should have been a true novice had I heeded my uncle. But, as thou knowest, I will be a knight."

"Ay, and a bold one thou wilt be," was the response; "as bold as our lord who is in France."

All day they held slowly on their way, and, though they frequently met other travellers, they attracted no more attention than an occasional curious glance. And toward sundown they came to the town of Dunstable.

"Now," cried Humphrey, joyfully, "here be a town. Let us make haste to enter before the curfew and find an inn. We have had a long fast."

"Shall we not rather go to the priory?" asked Hugo.

"Nay, verily," answered Humphrey. "I go to no priory to-night. I will go to an inn, and I will have there a mighty supper, and a good bed, and no priestly duties to perform. I know not how to perform them if I would. And I proclaim to no man that we be counterfeits. And moreover, the priests here may be even as the parish priest of Oundle. Mayhap he will not set the pursuers on our track, but I trust him not. I trust no man who sendeth forth travellers with such a breakfast." So saying, he rode boldly down the main street which he had entered till he came to where it intersected another main street at right angles. There he stopped. "Here be inns in plenty," he said. "It must be this town is on the Watling Street." And he questioned the groom who came to take their tired horses.

"Yea," answered the groom. "This be the town of Dunstable. And here it is that the Watling Street crosseth the Icknield Street."

"*Pax vobiscum*," said Humphrey. "I will in to the fire and my supper. Do thou care well for the beasts." And, followed by Hugo, he strode off with a gait which was not often seen on a priest.

The inn which Humphrey had chosen displayed the sign of the Shorn Lamb, and was one of the smallest in the neighborhood; it made its patrons at home in its large kitchen while they waited for the meal to be served. There was but one other guest in the room when Hugo and Humphrey entered, and the moment the faithful serving-man saw him he was grateful for his priest's garb; for the fierce little man who was giving orders in a peremptory manner was none other than Walter Skinner.

In great fear he had fled from Newark at the instance of the courtier, but his courage, after three days of wandering, had returned to him; for his hope of one day being a duke died hard. "Though I be the king's spy no longer," he had said to himself, "I have been the king's spy. Therefore I have had a certain measure of preferment and may hope for more." And in this humor he had come into Dunstable by way of the Icknield

Street, and by chance had chosen the very inn Humphrey had selected. That he had fled from Newark and was no longer in pursuit of them Humphrey did not know; and he, accordingly, withdrew deeper into the concealment of his hood, while Hugo did the same.

As for Walter Skinner, he looked at them with contempt. "Here cometh a beggarly priest and a novice," he thought, "to keep company at the table with me. I will none of it." And he said haughtily to the innkeeper: "Worthy host, I have no liking to priests. Seat them not at the table with me. Give me thy company, if it please thee, but serve the priest and his novice elsewhere."

The innkeeper happened to be in a surly humor. Certain affairs had gone contrary and vexed him. Therefore he made answer: "I keep but one table. There may ye all feed or ye may look elsewhere. There be other inns." And he added slowly and impressively, "They - be - all - full - also."

"Why, here be a circumstance!" cried Walter Skinner. "The inns of this town be full, sayest thou? Why, all the inns in London be not full, I warrant thee. And why should they be full here in this bit of a town, with one street running this way, and one another way, like a cross? I would have thee to know that I have been servant to the king, and am used to be served accordingly."

"And what service hast thou done the king?" demanded the surly innkeeper, unbelievingly.

"I did watch from the top of the high tree the De Aldithely castle," was the boastingly given answer. "I did see the young lord and his serving-man flee through the postern and enter the wood." He was about to rehearse all the particulars of his pursuit of the runaways when the innkeeper interrupted him.

"Thou must, then," said he, "be the spy for whom the king is looking, and I will give thee to him."

"Nay, nay," said Walter Skinner, his fierceness all gone as he suddenly remembered the warning given him in Newark by the courtier who had set him free. "That thou mayest not do. I do journey toward the south. Thou mayest not delay me."

"I could if I would," returned the innkeeper, his surly mood vanishing as he saw before him the opportunity of enjoying himself by tormenting somebody. "But thou art such a sprat of a man that my compassion forbids me. The king looketh for thee to hear thee tell what thou knowest of the whereabouts of the young lord and his companion. If thou canst not tell, he will have thy head; so hath he sworn. For he is in an evil rage, and heads are as nothing to him when he rageth, as thou knowest. He searcheth also for the bailiff who had thee in charge and let thee escape. I warrant thee the bailiff hath a wit too sound to go proclaiming how he was some great man, even a bailiff in the town of Newark."

All this was lost on Walter Skinner, however, who grasped but one thought, that he was in danger, and had but one anxiety, how to escape it. He turned now with some degree of humility to Humphrey.

"What!" said the innkeeper. "Dost thou turn to the beggarly priest whom thou erstwhile didst despise? But it shall not avail thee. It is with me that thou must deal. Knowest thou that I might lose my head for harboring thee, if I give thee not up? But I will hide thee, my little sprat, so that the king himself would not know thee. Come with me."

The little spy, his importance all gone, did as the burly innkeeper bade him, and Hugo and Humphrey were left alone in the kitchen with the servants.

"What do we?" asked Humphrey, in a low tone. "Flee?"

"Nay," replied Hugo. "That were to invite pursuit."

"This innkeeper is a knave," said Humphrey.

"The more reason for caution," answered Hugo.

"I have heard that some priests be great sleepers and great eaters," said Humphrey a few moments later.

"Some priests be," agreed Hugo.

"Then I be one of them. I do now drowse in my chair, and naught but the call to supper shall awake me. And then will I play so busily with my food that no words can escape me save *pax vobiscum.* This rascal innkeeper learns naught of me."

Presently back came the innkeeper with Walter Skinner in his turn playing scullion. "Here, sir priest," cried the innkeeper. "Here is he who shall serve thee at thy meal."

But there was no response. The priest's head was sunk

on his breast, and he seemed asleep. His novice also appeared to sleep.

The innkeeper, emboldened, now gazed openly and curiously at the two. "They have not come far," he said to himself. "Their garments be not travel-stained enough for that. They be some dullards of small wit on their first journey, for the groom did say they knew not that this was Dunstable."

His observations were here cut short by the appearance of three other travellers; but their entrance failed to arouse the priest and his novice, who remained, as before, apparently asleep.

"Yea, verily," thought the innkeeper, as he slowly advanced to meet the newcomers, "they be but two dullards. There is neither game nor gain to be made of them as there is of this Walter Skinner, from whom I will take his horse before I let him go. I will e'en bid priest and novice pack to make room for these newcomers, from whom I may win something, and to save room for others who may come."

Accordingly he set to work, but it was with great difficulty that he roused the two. "*Pax vobiscum,*" murmured Humphrey, sleepily. "Is the supper ready?"

"Yea, but at some other inn," returned the innkeeper. "Here be three worthy people just come in. There is not room for them and ye. The groom bringeth your horses, and ye must go." Without a word of objection Hugo and Humphrey rose to do the innkeeper's bidding and depart. But they walked like men half awake, and followed the innkeeper stumblingly; and mounted their horses clumsily, to the great merriment of the groom. It was now dark, and they knew not which way to turn. "I choose not another inn," said Humphrey, "though we bide supperless in the streets."

"Then choose I," returned Hugo. And he rode off down the street with Humphrey close beside him.

"Lad, lad!" cried the serving-man, "thou must not lead. It will betray us."

At once Hugo fell behind, and the two rode on until, at a little inn called the Blue Bell, the boy bade the serving-man stop. The two alighted, gave their horses to the groom, went in, were promptly served a good supper, and, in due time, were shown to their beds.

"There be dangers on the Watling Street as well as in the fen," said Humphrey.

In the meanwhile the keeper of the Shorn Lamb was having his enjoyment at the expense of Walter Skinner. He bade him serve the three strangers and fear nothing, as no one would recognize him in the guise of a scullion.

"Why, here didst thou come strutting it finely," said the innkeeper, in a mocking tone. "And dost thou strut now? Nay, verily; but thou art as meek as any whipped cock. And since it was by thy strut that men did recognize thee, how shall they make thee out when thy fine strut is gone? Wherefore serve the strangers, and be not afraid."

In spite of this exhortation the manner of Walter Skinner still betrayed doubt, and even timidity. And at last he made the innkeeper understand that it was he whom he feared and not the strangers.

The innkeeper laughed. "Dost fear me?" he said. "Why, thou needst not - that is, thou needst not if thou observest my conditions. Thou hast a horse that thou needest not, since thou hast legs of thine own. Somewhat short they be, and somewhat stiff in the joints, being more made to strut with than for the common gait of mankind. Still I doubt not they will carry thee whither thou wouldst go after I have dismissed thee. Serve the strangers, therefore, and afterward thou shalt sup."

In great meekness Walter Skinner obeyed, and the innkeeper, observing him, sat down later with satisfaction to his own meal.

Now it chanced that the strangers had ordered liquor, and Walter Skinner paused in the bringing of it long enough to take a drink of it and fill up the measure again with water. And in a few moments his fears were gone. He surreptitiously drank again, and yet again, for the strangers were convivial. And, by the time they were served and his task done, he had forgotten his danger and remembered only the injustice of the innkeeper.

"What!" he said to himself. "Here be a degradation! Here be a putting of fine metal to base uses! I who have been servant to the king am made a scullion to traveling strangers who be drunken, moreover, and fit only to be served by this rascal innkeeper who hath made a scullion of me. And shall he have my horse also? Nay, he shall not. I will away to the stables this moment and set out and gain my liberty."

Nobody noticed him as he went out the kitchen door, and nobody saw him as he entered the stable and prepared his horse for the journey. And, still unnoticed, he mounted, after many a crazy lurch, and set off down the street. In due time he came to the gate, and the watchman challenged him.

"Dost stop me, sirrah!" demanded the half-drunken Walter Skinner. "I be the servant of the king; and, moreover, I be but just come from the inn of the Shorn Lamb. Pass me outside the walls."

The watchman, at the mention of the Shorn Lamb, made haste to lead the horse through the narrow side gate, for he and the innkeeper were confederates in villany; and away went Walter Skinner at a great pace toward London.

CHAPTER XXI

Knowing nothing of the escape of their old enemy, Hugo and Humphrey arose the next morning and, after paying their reckoning, departed without having incurred the suspicion of any one in the town.

"This cometh of leaving the inn of the Shorn Lamb in good season," observed Humphrey, with satisfaction.

"I did think we were put out of the inn," said Hugo, demurely.

"Ay, lad," agreed Humphrey; "thou art right. If all who go to the Shorn Lamb were thus put out, and so did leave in good season, there would be fewer lambs abroad without their fleece. Didst see Walter Skinner in the guise of the scullion?"

"Yea," answered Hugo.

"If I be so good a priest as he is a scullion, I fear detection from no man. Why, he doth look to be a good scullion, whereas when he is clad as the king's spy, he looketh a very poor spy; and he doth act the part moreover very lamentably. We had come badly off had he been as good a spy as he is a scullion."

"Ay, and had he been less drunken," said Hugo.

"Thou hast well said, lad," agreed Humphrey. "Let a man that would have ill success in what he undertaketh but befuddle his wit with drink, and ill success he will have, and that in good measure. And the scorn and contempt of his fellows, moreover, even as hath this little spy."

"And yet," observed Hugo, thoughtfully, "it were hard to find a man who is not at some time drunken."

"Hadst thou that from thine uncle, the prior?" asked Humphrey, quickly. "Or didst thou gain it from thine own very ancient experience?"

"Now I have angered thee," said Hugo, frankly.

"Yea, lad, thou hast. This is a time of great drinking, that I know; but never have I seen my lord drunken. And never hath any man seen me drunken, nor my father, nor my grandsire. There be ever enough sober ones in the worst of times to keep the world right side uppermost. And that thou wilt find when thou hast lived to be forty years old. But thou art but fourteen, and I am foolish to be angered with thee for what is, after all, but lack of experience. How soon come we to this St. Albans?"

"Why, it is but thirteen miles from Dunstable," answered Hugo, pleasantly.

"Then may we pass it by without stopping," cried Humphrey, joyfully. "And how much farther on lieth London?"

"Twenty miles," replied Hugo.

Gulielma Zollinger

"Then do we rest in London to-night, if we may," said Humphrey. "Our horses be not of the best, but neither are they of the worst; and it were an ill beast that could not go thirty-three miles before sunset on the Watling Street."

"Ay," agreed Hugo. "But we may not ride too fast, else shall we arouse wonder."

Humphrey sighed. "Thou art right, lad," he said. "And wonder might lead to questions, and questions to a stopping of our journey. For how know I what answer to make to questions that I be not looking for? I will therefore go more slowly."

The road was now by no means empty of passengers. Trains of packhorses were going down to London. And just as they reached St. Albans came a nobleman with his retinue, going down to his town house in London. "So might my lord ride, but for the wicked king," said Humphrey, in a low tone, as they stood aside. Then passing into the city of St. Albans, they at once sought an inn and made the early hour suit them for dinner that so they might journey on the sooner.

They had entered St. Albans in the rear of the nobleman's party. They passed out of it an hour later unnoticed in a throng of people. "And now," said Humphrey, looking back at the town on the slope, "let the priest at Oundle play us false if he like; we be safely through the town."

"It was near here that the Saxon pope, Adrian IV, was born," observed Hugo.

"Ay, lad," answered Humphrey, indifferently. "But I be

nearing the place where I be a priest no longer. If we may not make too much haste, let us turn aside in the wood and find a hut where they will take us in for the night, and where, perchance, I may get a dream. 'Tis a mighty place, this London, and I would fain see what 'twere best to do."

Hugo made no objection, and when they were within ten miles of the great city they turned their horses to the left and sought shelter in Epping Forest.

"I like the wood," observed Humphrey, with satisfaction. "It seemeth a safer place than the Watling Street; for who knoweth what rascals ride thereon, and who be no more what they seem than we be ourselves?"

"Why, so they be no worse than we, we need not fear," returned Hugo, with a smile.

But Humphrey was not to be convinced. "I be forty years old," he said, "and what be safer than a tree but many trees? And the grass is under foot, and the sky above, and naught worse than robbers and wardens to be feared in the wood."

Hugo laughed. "And what worse than robbers on the Watling Street?" he asked.

"King's men, lad, king's men. A good honest robber of the woods will take but thy purse or other goods; but the king's man will take thee, and the king will take, perchance, thy life. I like not the Watling Street, nor care to see it more."

They were now going slowly through the wood in a

bridle-path, one behind the other. Presently they came out into a glade, and across it, peeping from amid the trees, they descried a hut. "That be our inn for the night, if they will take us," said Humphrey, decisively. And, crossing the glade, he rode boldly up to the door and knocked.

The hut was very small and was made of wattle and daub. A faint line of smoke was coming from a hole in the roof. The knock with the end of Humphrey's stick was a vigorous one. Nevertheless it went so long without answer that he knocked again, and this time with better success. The door opened slowly a little way, and through the aperture thus made an old and withered face looked out.

"What wilt thou?" asked a cracked, high voice.

"Entrance and shelter for the night," replied Humphrey, promptly and concisely.

The door opened a little wider and the man within stepping outside, his person was revealed. He was of medium height and spare, and he wore a long gray tunic of wool reaching to his knees. Beneath this garment his lean legs were bare, while on his feet he wore shoes of skin which reached to the ankle, and which were secured by thongs. Such as he Hugo and Humphrey had often seen, but never before a face like his, in which craftiness and credulity were strangely mingled. For several minutes he stood there, first scrutinizing Humphrey and then Hugo.

At last Humphrey grew impatient. "Do we come in, or do we stay out?" he demanded.

"Why, that I hardly know," was the slow answer. "There be many rogues about; some in priests' robes and some not."

"Yea, verily," responded Humphrey, fervently; "but we be not of the number. *Pax vobiscum*," he added, hastily. "I had well nigh forgot that," he said in an aside to Hugo.

But the old man's ears were keen, and he caught the aside meant for Hugo's ears alone. "Thou be but a sorry priest to forget thy *pax vobiscum*," he said with a crafty look. "Perchance thou art no priest," he added, coming closer and peering into Humphrey's face.

He looked so long that Humphrey again grew impatient. "What seest thou on my face?" he asked.

"Why, I do see a mole on thy nose. It is a very small one, and of scant size, but because thou hast it thou mayest come down from thy horse, thou and the lad with thee, and I will give thee lodging for the night."

Instinctively Humphrey raised his hand and touched a tiny mole on the side and near the end of his nose. The man of the hut watched him. "I see thou knowest that a mole near the end of the nose is lucky," he said.

"Not I," declared Humphrey. "I had not before heard of such a thing."

The man of the hut regarded him pityingly. Then he said: "Come down from thy horse, thou unwitting lucky one, and come thou and the lad within while I do hide thy horses in a thick, for I would share thy luck. Dost not know that to show kindness to a lucky one is to share his fortune? Thou hadst not come within the hut but for thy mole, I warrant thee. For I do know that thou art the false priest and the young lord from Oundle that stopped not at St. Albans as ye were bid."

Hugo and Humphrey looked at each other. Then Humphrey said, "I know not, after all, whether to come in or not."

"Come in! come in!" cried the old man, eagerly. "I must share thy luck, and that could I not do if I played thee false. Come in!"

Still hesitating, Humphrey glanced about him. He knew not who might be on his track. And then he decided to go in.

"No matter who knocketh while I be gone," said the old man, earnestly, "give heed to none. Only when I come and knock four times: one for thee, one time for the lad, and two times for the two horses, which signifieth that I know ye; listen close. And when I say 'mole,' open the door softly and not over wide."

Humphrey, who with Hugo was now within the hut, promised to obey, and the old man, closing the door after him, departed with the horses.

At once Humphrey put out the smoking embers of the fire burning on the earthen floor in the centre of the hut. "If any knock and see the smoke and hear no answer, will they not break in the door?" he said.

The old man had been gone but a short time when a tramp of horses was heard. The riders paused before the door of the hut as Humphrey had done, and one of them knocked heavily upon it with his stick. But there was no answer. Again there came a knock and a cry, "Open, old Bartlemy!"

Meanwhile, old Bartlemy had come creeping cautiously back, and from behind a screen of vines which hung from an oak beheld them. "Ay, ye may knock and cry," he muttered craftily; "but which one of ye hath a mole near the end of his nose? Not one of ye. Therefore I will have none of ye. And ye may be gone."

"The old rascal groweth deaf," said one of the riders.

"Nay," answered the second. "There cometh no smoke out of the roof. He is doubtless from home for the night."

Old Bartlemy hastily glanced toward the roof of the hut. He had left a smouldering fire, and now no fire was there. "The false priest hath put it out," he said joyfully. "Now know I that he hath luck with him, and I will serve him faithfully. Ay, knock!" he continued. "Knock thy fill. I did but now hear thee call me 'old rascal,' though I have helped thee to thy desires many times, for which thou didst pay me by ever threatening to bring the ranger upon me for the game I take to keep me alive. Thou wantest naught of old Bartlemy but to further thine own schemes."

There was silence a moment, and then the first speaker said, "The priest of Oundle hath cheaply bought his altar cloth if we find not these two. We know they be between St. Albans and London. And we do know they be, for the present, gone from the Watling Street, for the carter from London whom we did meet did tell us that he had met them not on the way. Therefore go thou to London by way of the Ermine Street, while I go down by the Watling Street. They may be now straying about in the wood, but we shall have them on one road or the other as they go into the city. The false priest rideth a gray, and the young lord a black. We shall have them without Bartlemy's aid, fear not."

Then the riders withdrew, each going his way, and Bartlemy a few moments later knocked on the door of the hut and was admitted by Humphrey. At once the old man made up the fire in the centre of the hut again.

"What doest thou?" demanded Humphrey. "Wouldst have other visitors?"

"Do not thou fear," responded Bartlemy. "Am I not here? And can I not hide thee and the lad beneath yon heap of rushes if a stranger come? No man will look for thee here. They that seek thee think that Bartlemy will aid them; and so he would but for thy mole. I be an old man, and never yet hath fortune come my way, and all because I did not before meet thee. For it hath been foretold me that a man having a mole near the end of his nose would bring me fortune. Wherefore I cleave to thee, and will protect thee with my life, if need be." So saying, he threw another fagot on the fire and, from a hidden cupboard, brought out a substantial meal of venison and bread. When the meal was finished he commanded: "Lie down and rest now, thou and the lad, while I keep watch. Thou wilt need thy wits on the morrow."

Humphrey reflected. Then he turned to Hugo. "Lie down, lad," he said kindly. "The old man is crazed when he talketh of moles, but he is right when he saith we have need of our wits on the morrow. And that meaneth we must rest in faith to-night."

The old man smiled triumphantly. "I be not so crazed as thou thinkest, neither," he said. "Thy mole is not only thy good fortune, but mine also." With that he put the remains of the meal back in the cupboard, shut the door, and replenished the fire. He then threw himself down on the earthen floor beside it, and lay there grinning and grimacing at the flames till Hugo and Humphrey fell asleep. A dozen times before dawn old Bartlemy rose to bend over the two, grinning and grimacing as he did so, and clasping his hands in ecstasy. But when the two awoke he was gone.

Humphrey, when he discovered Bartlemy's absence, started up in alarm. "I did get no dream, lad," he said to Hugo, whom his movements had aroused; "and the old man is gone. I know not what to do."

CHAPTER XXII

An hour went by and still old Bartlemy did not come; an hour of silence broken only by occasional whispers between Hugo and Humphrey.

Then the old man softly opened the door and stood smiling before them.

"Thou didst think me false, is it not so?" he said, addressing Humphrey and casting an affectionate glance as he did so on the small mole near the end of the Saxon's nose.

Great as was his anxiety, Hugo could but laugh to see how the serving-man was placed before himself, and all on account of an unfortunate blemish on his countenance. And his enjoyment was heightened by the embarrassment and half-concealed irritation it occasioned Humphrey.

But old Bartlemy paid no attention to Hugo and his merry mood. He proceeded with despatch to set out the morning meal from the hidden cupboard. "Eat well and heartily," he exhorted both his guests; "for so shall ye be able to set your enemies at defiance. A full stomach giveth a man courage and taketh him through many dangers. But why," he continued, addressing Humphrey solicitously, "why shouldest thou have many dangers? Why dost thou not let the young lord ride forth alone?"

Humphrey's answer was a look so full of indignation that the old man ventured to say nothing more, except, "I see that thou art not to be persuaded, and I will e'en help ye both."

So saying, he went outside and brought in a bundle or pack which he had, on his return to the hut, secreted in a convenient hiding-place. "I have been to a spot I wot of," he began, "and there did I borrow this raiment. I did borrow it, I say, and ye must put it on. When ye have no further need of it, then I will return it to its owner."

Humphrey gazed at him in astonishment. At last he said, "Thou knowest that we journey hence this morn and shall see thee no more. What meanest thou?"

"Why, this," was the response. "I go with thee."

"Thou goest with me!" repeated Humphrey.

"Ay," was the stubborn answer. "Thinkest thou I will lightly part with him who is decreed to make my fortune? Thou art the man the fortune-teller spake to me of. 'Cleave to him that hath a mole near the end of his nose,' saith the fortune-teller, and I will of a surety do so. But tell me truly, should the young lord be captured, would thy ability to make my fortune be diminished?"

"Yea, verily," answered Humphrey, positively. "Were my dear lad captured, I could do nothing for thee."

"Thou needst say no more," said the old man, for the first time that morning looking full at Hugo. "He seemeth a good lad. I will protect him also with my life, if need be. For what will a man not do if he may thereby escape the marring of his fortune?"

Old Bartlemy now ceased speaking and devoted all his energies to hastily undoing the bundle he had brought in, and sorting out a portion of what it contained.

"What hast thou there?" asked Humphrey, contemptuously, as he pointed to a woman's robe, tunic, and hood of green. "Here be no fine ladies."

"Nay, speak not so fast," replied old Bartlemy, stubbornly. "Thy young lord will don these things, and then shalt thou see a fair lady on a journey bent."

Hugo flushed. "I wear no woman's dress," he said with determination.

"Why, how now?" demanded old Bartlemy. "Art thou better than Longchamp, bishop of Ely? When he did flee he fled as a woman, and in a green tunic and hood, moreover. When thou art as old as thou now art young, thou wilt welcome the means that helpeth thee safely on." The old man's manner was so changed from that of the night before, and he displayed so much energy, foresight, and knowledge, that Hugo and Humphrey looked at each other in wonder. He was still old, but he was no longer senile.

"Knowest thou not," he continued, "that the king's men look for thee either as the young lord or as the false priest's novice? Dally no longer, but put on this woman's garb."

"Yea, lad," counselled Humphrey, "put it on. It will suit thee better than the king's dungeon."

Thus urged, Hugo obeyed, and presently was stepping about the hut most discontentedly in the guise of a woman. "Stride not so manfully or we be undone," cried old Bartlemy. "Canst thou not mince thy gait? There! That hath a more seemly look."

The pack he had brought in was very large, and from it he now took the garments and armor of an esquire, which he handed to Humphrey. "When thou shalt don these," he said, "it will come to pass that thou hast been sent to bring thy young lady safe to London town."

With alacrity Humphrey tossed aside his priest's robe and clad himself in what old Bartlemy offered him. "Now may I forget my *pax vobiscum* and no harm be done," he exclaimed joyfully.

Hugo could but smile at the pride and pleasure of Humphrey's manner as he arrayed himself. "Ah, my good Humphrey!" he cried; "I have found thee out. Thou wouldst be an esquire, even as I would be a knight."

Humphrey sighed. "Yea, lad," he confessed, "but I am but a Saxon serving-man."

Like a hawk the little old man was watching both. "And I have found thee out," he said, turning to Hugo. "The mole on his nose doth signify the good fortune thou wilt bring him, even as it signifieth what he will do for me. Be sure, gentle lady, I shall serve thee well."

Hugo laughed and, in his character of lady, inclined his head courteously.

Humphrey, who could not for a moment forget the business in hand, ignored this pleasantry and inquired curtly: "But how goest thou with us, Bartlemy? Will not the men who were here last night know thee?"

"Nay, verily," replied Bartlemy. "I have a friend to my counsel that they know not of. 'Tis he who did lend these disguises, and did instruct me, moreover, in many matters. He did bid me overcome the young lord's objections to wearing woman's dress by naming Longchamp and his green tunic and hood. And many other matters he hath helped me to, even the whole conduct of the journey, as thou shalt presently see." With one last look at Humphrey's nose he backed out of the hut and made off in a surprisingly agile manner for one of his age.

"Now a plague upon his foolishness!" exclaimed Humphrey. "I had all but forgotten my nose, but he will be ever bringing it to my mind. Yet, if the mole on it take us safely through London, I complain not. And I do hope he forget not his instructions and become again upon our hands the witless old man of last night." He advanced to the door and glanced out. "But here come two horses and a mule," he continued. "Whose they be, I know not, nor what hath been done with ours."

Hugo at this also looked out the door. "In size and in gait these horses be ours," he said.

"Yea, lad; but what should be thy black is a rusty brown with a star in his forehead and one white foot.

And what should be my gray is that same rusty brown with two white feet and a patch on his side. And the tails of both be bobbed, and the manes cropped, and the saddles and housings be different. This is more of Bartlemy's 'friend to his counsel,' perchance. And I hope his friend be not the Evil One." He paused a moment. "Seest thou the old woman on the mule that leadeth the horses?" he continued.

"That is Bartlemy," replied Hugo.

"Ay," agreed Humphrey. "But we had not known it had we not been made ready for mysteries. He looketh like an ancient crone, and will be thy old nurse, no doubt, going with thee on thy journey. Well, they be wise men that would know the five of us."

"Five?" questioned Hugo.

"Ay, lad. Thou and Bartlemy and I and the two horses. Perchance the mule is honest and what he seemeth to be."

Bartlemy, having tied the animals, now came up to the door of the hut in great exultation. "What thinkest thou of these strange horses, Humphrey?" he asked.

"I do think they lack their tails," answered Humphrey, gravely, "which is a sad lack in summer."

The old man grinned. "And what more thinkest thou?" he asked.

"I do think they have need of manes also," was the reply.

With an air of pride the old man, clad in his woman's dress, consisting of a long, loose, blue robe surmounted by a long, red head-rail which reached to his knees, walked back to the horses. "Come hither," he said to Humphrey. "It were not well to cut off what one may need before it grow again. Seest thou how only the outside of the tail is cut so as to bush out over what is braided fine in many strands and caught up cunningly beneath? And come hither. Seest thou how the mane is cunningly looped and gummed, so that it seemeth to be short, when a dip in the stream will make it long again? And this brown is but a stain, and the white patches a bleach that will last but till the horse sheds again."

"This is the work of thy friend?" inquired Humphrey, gravely.

"Yea," answered old Bartlemy, jubilantly.

"And he is an honest man?"

Old Bartlemy frowned. "He is my friend. And he hath served thee well, if he hath kept thee and the lad from the hands of the king. Ask no more. He had not done so much, but that I did tell him it was to make my fortune. And now mount, my esquire! mount, my gentle lady! and I, thy nurse, will mount. And we will all away to London town." "By which road?" asked Humphrey, reining in his stained and bleached horse.

"By the Watling Street," was the confident answer.

Humphrey seemed dissatisfied. Seeing which the old man said: "Why, we must e'en go by the Watling Street or the Ermine Street, since we have the young lady here in charge. Such is the custom of travellers to go by one or the other."

"I like not the Watling Street," objected Humphrey.

"Didst hear the men at the door of my hut?" asked old Bartlemy, earnestly.

"Yea," replied Humphrey, briefly.

"Didst note how he who watcheth for us on the Watling Street did tell his plans in a voice that all might hear?"

"Yea."

"Therefore I go by the Watling Street and not by the Ermine Street," said old Bartlemy, with determination. "He that hath so little discretion that he telleth his plans in the ears of all who may listen is less to be feared than he that sayeth little. He that watcheth for us on the Ermine Street hath keen eyes and a silent tongue. Therefore go we by the Watling Street and, moreover, the friend to my counsel hath bid me so to do. I warrant thee more than one priest will be stopped there, while the esquire and the young lady and the nurse escape notice."

"Mayhap thou art right," agreed Humphrey, after some reflection.

Bartlemy did not wait to answer, but, giving his mule a slap with the reins, set forward, and in a moment all three were crossing the glade, whence they followed the same bridle-path by which Hugo and Humphrey had come the day before, and so gained the Watling

Street. Many people were upon it, and Bartlemy, following the instructions of him who had planned for him, managed to ride near enough to a merchant's party to be mistaken as members of it by an unthinking observer.

In his garb of esquire Humphrey was more at home than in that of the priest, and he looked boldly about him. "Here be a strange thing, lad," he said. "As we did come upon this road I did see a priest with his novice pass by. Seest thou that other near at hand? And looking back I see yet another. He that watcheth for us is like to have his hands full."

"Many priests be abroad," replied Hugo, with a smile. "It was to that the Canon Thurstan trusted when he sent us forth."

"He should, then, not have sent us to that rascally one at Oundle," growled Humphrey. "Speak not o'er much with the lady," cautioned old Bartlemy, riding up. "It is not seemly. Let her stay by me, her nurse. So hath the friend to my counsel instructed me."

At once Hugo fell back, reining his horse alongside the mule and a half pace in advance; whereat old Bartlemy smiled in approbation.

"Where go we in London?" asked Hugo, curiously.

"Thou shalt see in good time," answered Bartlemy. "It may be one place, it may be another. I can tell when we have passed him who watcheth for us. I know many places."

The old man, turning his face away, Hugo saw that he

did not wish to talk further, so he contented himself by seeing as much as he could with his keen young eyes of what went on before him, old Bartlemy having previously cautioned him against gazing about over much.

As they drew nearer the city the crowd became more dense, being swelled by those who were coming out of it on their way north. A little party of knights, esquires, pages, and ladies travelling at a faster pace overtook them, and so they were still better protected from observation than before, as the new party were now obliged, by the throng, to go forward slowly. So on they went till they came to the church of St. Andrew, and the Fleet River, and, crossing the bridge, found themselves, as old Bartlemy said, not far from the New Gate, through which they must enter the city. They had no sooner entered than old Bartlemy said to Hugo,

"Thou didst not see the man at the hut?"

"Nay," answered Hugo, with a nervous start.

"Yon at the entrance to the meat market opposite the Grey Friars is he. Seem not to notice him, but mark him well. He hath a bailiff to his help, and it will go hard with somebody."

"He stoppeth not that priest and his novice," observed Hugo.

"That is because the bailiff knoweth both and hath instructed him," answered Bartlemy. "Look downward now right modestly till we be safely past, for thou hast a speaking eye. Thou art not lucky like the good Humphrey, to have a dull eye, which seeth much and seemeth to see naught."

Hugo glanced down as he was bid, and soon they were past in safety. But Humphrey, half turning in his saddle and gazing back, saw a priest and his novice stopped. "And the priest rideth a gray and the novice a black," mused Humphrey, "which is a wonderful thing, and not to be accounted for except by chance."

CHAPTER XXIII

The pace at which Walter Skinner had left Dunstable for London he kept up for some two miles, when he slackened his rein at the bidding of his half-drunken fancy.

"I be for London town," he said to himself with a serious look. "And other men than I have been there before now. Yea, verily, and have got them safe home again into the bargain. But not so will I do. For in London will I bide, either till the king make a duke of me or till I become the Lord Mayor. For I be resolved to rise in the world. And the first step toward it is to be resolved; yea, and to be determined; and to look Dame Fortune full in the face and to say to her, 'Play no tricks on me.'"

By this time he was come up with a belated carrier who, since his cart was empty and he upon his return journey, dared to be upon the road at night. There was no moon, and in the starlight Walter Skinner could see but imperfectly. "And who art thou?" he demanded loftily, "that thou shouldest creak and rumble along over the road and block the way of a rising man? The sun doth rise, and why not I? Only the sun riseth not in the middle of the night, and neither will I. Nay, verily, but I will wait to rise till I be come to London town. And so I bid thee, whoever thou art, make place for me that I may pass thee upon the road."

The carter, wondering much who this drunken madman might be, made no answer but drove his creaking
vehicle forward slowly as before, and in the middle of
the highway. Behind him, and at the tail of the cart,
followed Walter Skinner with equal slowness. For
some moments he said nothing more as, with closed
eyes and heavily nodding head, he rode along. Then he
roused himself. "Stop!" he called fiercely. "Stop, I say.
I will go to bed in thy wagon or cart or whatever it may
be, which I cannot see for want of light."

"I carry not passengers for naught," observed the
carter, civilly.

"Yea, but thou wilt carry me," retorted Walter Skinner.
"I tell thee I serve the king. Why, the prior of St.
Edmund's did give me a horse when mine own was
gone, and wilt thou refuse me a bed? It shall go hard
with thee, varlet that thou art, if thou dost. I be ready to
sink from weariness. Lend me a hand down and into
thy cart; lead thou my horse, and so shall we proceed, I
at rest as becometh the king's man, and thou serving
me, thy proper master."

The carter was slow of wit, and, as most men did, he
trembled at the mention of the king. He therefore did
as he was requested, and Walter Skinner was soon
bumping along the road, oblivious to all his surroun-
dings. In the cart he might have remained until he
reached St. Albans, but that, just at dawn, he had a
frightful dream. He was again at Dunstable, and the
landlord of the Shorn Lamb was about to deliver him
to the king who stood, in his dream, a hideous monster
with horns upon his head. In a shiver of dread he

awoke. The cart was standing still, and, at the side of the road, reposed the carter overcome by sleep. By his side lay his drinking-horn. With trembling limbs Walter Skinner climbed down from the cart. Then, seizing the carter's horn, he untied his horse, which was fastened to the tail of the cart, and mounted; took from the horn a long drink, and once more set out at a furious pace which shortly became once more a slow one. Pausing only long enough at St. Albans to procure breakfast for himself and a feed for his horse, he continued on to London which he reached late in the afternoon. But he did not go in at New Gate, for, making a sharp turn at St. Andrew's, he went south till he came to Fleet street, when, turning to the left, he entered the city through Lud Gate. Clad in his scullion's garb, and with his face flushed from drink he presented a strange appearance as he permitted his horse to carry him whither he would through the narrow streets.

"Here be people enough," he said to himself, "and yea, verily, here be noise enough. But I will stop all that when I be Lord Mayor. What! shall mine ears ring with vile din? If so be I would speak to my horse could he hear me? Nay, that he could not. When I be Lord Mayor no smith shall strike on anvil in my presence. And when I pass by, let the carpenters cease to drive their nails; let all the armorers cease their hammering; let the coopers forbear to hoop their casks; and then can I gather my wits together, which is more than I can now do." He was right as to the din; for here in these narrow lanes the craftsmen lived and worked. Each one had his tenement of one room above and one below. In the one below he worked, or in the street, and in the room above he dwelt with his family.

As he went uncertainly up one of these narrow lanes and down another, leading north or south out of Cheapside, as the case might be, the rabble began to gather about him and to bait him with jeers of various sorts.

"Why, how now!" he exclaimed, when he had once more come into Cheapside. And he put on his fiercest air, which sat strangely enough on one clad as a scullion. "Do ye gibe and jeer at me who am servant to the king? What know ye of young runaway lords and Saxon serving-men? And the perils of a long way, and the keeper of the Shorn Lamb? I could open your eyes for ye, if I thought it worth my while. But ye be all base-born knaves -"

The last words were but out of his mouth when a strong hand jerked him to the ground. And, not seeing what he did, as he struck fiercely out, his clenched fist landed on the chest of the warden who was passing, and Walter Skinner was promptly seized and about to be haled off to punishment.

Cheapside was the principal market-place of London. It was broad, and bordered on each side by booths or sheds for the sale of merchandise. A sudden disturbance attracted the attention of the bailiff who held Walter Skinner. And, even as he turned his head to look, the very man that had dragged Walter Skinner from his horse detached the little man from the grasp of the careless officer, and bade him flee. "Flee away, thou half-drunken scullion," said his liberator. "Thou dost lack thy wits, and so I would not have thee also lack thy liberty."

Now Walter Skinner was in that condition when,

although he could not walk straight, he could run. And away he went, his first impetus carrying him well down into Bow Lane, which opened from Cheapside to the south, where he speedily brought up against a curb post and fell into the gutter. His appearance was not improved when he rose, but he started again, and took this time, not the curb post, but a stout farmer. The farmer instinctively bracing himself to meet the shock of Walter Skinner's fall against him, no harm was done; but he whirled round, grasped the little terrified rascal by the shoulder, and hurried him into the adjacent inn yard. "Had I been an old woman or a young child I might have been sprawling in the gutter," he began severely, "and all because of thee. What account givest thou of thyself?"

"Thou art but a yeoman," returned Walter Skinner, disdainfully. "And dost thou ask me to account to thee? Account thou to me, sirrah. What didst thou in the street standing there like a gutter post to obstruct the way of passengers in haste? But for thee I had been well sped on my way."

The farmer heard him in amazement. Then he said: "I do perceive that thou art a fool; and with fools I never meddle." And seizing him once more by the shoulder, he thrust him into the street. "Speed on thy way, little braggart," he said, "even till thou comest to thy master, who must be the Evil One himself."

Walter Skinner sped away, by degrees slacking his pace till, after much wandering, he came to a low public house on Thames Street, where he slipped in, hid himself in a corner, and went fast asleep. It was noon of the next day before he was discovered and routed out by a tapster. " This be no place for a scullion," said the tapster. "Get to thy duties."

"I be no scullion," retorted Walter Skinner, indignantly. "Till now I was the king's man with good hope
to be a duke or the mayor of London."

"I go to tell master of thee," returned the tapster. "And
he will set thee to scour knives in a trice."

The tapster was as good as his word, and Walter
Skinner, much against his will, was soon at work.
"Here be another degradation," he muttered over his
knife blades, "and I stand it not. I be not so mean-
spirited as to labor, nor to do the bidding of other men
who should do mine." So saying, he stole from the
kitchen and the house into the streets, where he
became a vagabond, and so remained, along with
thousands of others like unto him.

Meanwhile Hugo and Humphrey and old Bartlemy
were having troubles of their own. The places in
London suitable for them to stop at which old
Bartlemy knew proved to be known to him by report
only. And, lacking the present help of him whom
Humphrey was pleased to call Bartlemy's "friend to his
counsel," the whole party soon knew not where to go;
for the old man had lost the energy with which he had
escorted them to London, and seemed to have sunk
back into the semi-helpless mixture of shrewdness and
credulity which he appeared when Hugo and Humphrey had first met him. One thing, and one only,
seemed to engross most of his attention, and that was
Humphrey's mole. And he was ever prating of the
fortune it was sure to bring him.

"Lad," said Humphrey at last, when they had been two

days in the town, "if we are to come safely off we must be rid of him. The gumming up of the horses' manes and the braiding of their tails have already made the innkeeper look strangely at us. Had he not set it down as the trick of some malicious groom, it had been worse for us. And I do fear the old man's babbling tongue. I will sound him to see how much will content him, and perchance from thy pouch and mine the sum may be made up."

Old Bartlemy was growing weary of his woman's dress, and weary of hovering around Hugo in the assumed capacity of his nurse. He was not in his apartment when Humphrey went to seek him, and further search revealed the fact that he was not in the house. So, somewhat disturbed, Humphrey went forth to find him, taking with him in his bosom Hugo's pouch as well as his own. The inn where they were now stopping was the White Horse in Lombard Street, and as Humphrey issued forth into the street he knew not which way to turn. "The old nurse did go south toward the waterside," volunteered a groom, who observed Humphrey's hesitation. "She seemeth like one that lacketh wit, and so I did keep a watch upon her till she went beyond my sight."

Humphrey flung the groom a penny and went south himself at a good gait. "If he be not at some public house I shall find him at a cock-fighting, no doubt," said Humphrey to himself. It was now the second day of July and clear and warm. The streets were full of hucksters having for sale, besides their usual wares, summer fruits and vegetables. But to all their cries Humphrey turned a deaf ear as he pushed impatiently on, keeping a sharp lookout for old Bartlemy. And what was his amazement to come upon him at last at the river side clad, not as the nurse, but in his own proper character.

"How now!" exclaimed Humphrey, with a frown. "Where is thy woman's garb? And what meanest thou to cast it aside in this manner?"

The old man peered up at him with a sly look on his face. "Ay, thou mayest storm," he said; "but if I be tired of woman's garb, what is that to thee?"

"Why, this," returned Humphrey. "Thou dost endanger our heads by this change."

The old man shook his head and smiled a silly smile. "Nay," he made answer. "I would not endanger thy head, for that would endanger the mole upon thy nose, and so my fortune. Thou doest me wrong."

Humphrey looked at him attentively and saw that a temporary weakness of mind due to his age had overtaken him. So he said in a soothing tone: "Where didst thou leave thy nurse's garb? I pray thee put it on again."

Again there came the sly look over the old man's withered face. "I do know where I did leave it," he said; "but I put it not on again. The friend I have to my counsel did bid me put it on, and I did obey him, for he is a magician. But I like it not, and I will wear it no more. Why, look thou," he continued earnestly. "When I wear it I must remain with the young lord, and be not free to consort with other men, and see and hear all that goeth on. Wherefore I will wear it no more."

Humphrey looked at him in despair. Then he said with

assumed cheerfulness: "I will now make thy fortune for thee. So mayest thou return to the wood while we journey on."

Old Bartlemy, as he listened, smiled with the delight of a child. "Said not the fortune-teller truly?" he cried. "And how much is my fortune that thou wilt make?"

"Why, that I hardly can tell," returned Humphrey. "What callest thou a fortune?"

Old Bartlemy looked at him craftily. "The friend to my counsel did say one hundred and fifty gold pieces, and that will pay for the disguises."

"No less?" asked Humphrey.

"Nay," returned old Bartlemy. "If thou dost leave me, I may never see the mole upon thy nose again. Therefore pay to me the one hundred and fifty gold pieces before I ask thee more. For the friend to my counsel did say, 'Take no less, and as much more as thou canst get.'"

"Thou art hard to content," said Humphrey. "But come thou to the nearest reputable inn, where we may be unwatched, and I will pay to thee the one hundred and fifty gold pieces which thou dost require. Should they of the street see thee receive it, thou wouldst not keep it long."

The old man, with a crafty shake of the head, followed along in Humphrey's wake. "I have the wit to keep my fortune," he said. "No man may wrest it from me."

Without further words Humphrey led the way, his mind full of anxious thoughts as to how he was to get himself, Hugo, and the horses away from the White Horse in Lombard Street without rousing suspicion when the mule of old Bartlemy was left behind and the old man himself in his character of nurse was missing. He was still busily thinking when they came to a respectable little inn called the Hart. Turning to old Bartlemy, who was following close behind, he said, "Here do we stop till I pay thee what thou hast asked."

Old Bartlemy said nothing, but he rubbed his hands together in delight, and kept so close to Humphrey that he almost trod on his heels.

"Now," said Humphrey, when they were alone and the old man had been paid, "I ask thee this grace, Bartlemy. Wilt thou not once more put on the nurse's garb and come back with me to the White Horse till I can pay the reckoning and get away? After that thou mayest cast it aside and wear it no more."

"Nay," replied old Bartlemy, jingling the gold pieces and looking at them with gloating eyes. "Nay, I will put on woman's dress no more."

"Not if I pay thee to do so?"

"Nay. I have here my fortune. What have I need of more?" And he sat down obstinately and became at once absorbed in counting over his gold pieces.

Humphrey, seeing that nothing was to be gained, and anxious for Hugo's welfare, at once left the room and the house and set out for the White Horse.

CHAPTER XXIV

Through the same crowded streets, and entirely unmindful of the people who jostled him, Humphrey mechanically pushed his way on his return journey. How should he and Hugo get away from the White Horse? He knew very little of the world, but this much he knew, that for them to attempt to leave with the old nurse missing would be to thoroughly arouse the suspicion which, so far, was half dormant.

"I will pay the reckoning now," he said to himself as he entered the inn yard. "And then we must do as we can to give them the slip. I know not why, but dreams be slow to come in this town. I would we were safely out of it."

He had but just paid it, and the innkeeper was about to inquire concerning his departure, when a great excitement arose. One of the frequent fires, for which the London of that day was noted, had broken out.

"A fire, sayest thou?" cried Humphrey.

"Yea," answered a groom, bursting into the bar. "A fire, master! A fire!"

Away ran the groom followed by the master. And Hugo coming down at this moment, Humphrey hurried

Gulielma Zollinger

to him. "Make haste, lad!" he cried. "Come with me to the stables. We must e'en serve ourselves and get out the horses and be off, ere the fire abate and the innkeeper and the grooms come back."

Hugo wondered, but said nothing, for he saw that Humphrey was greatly excited. And with despatch the horses were saddled and led out. "I would not that people lose their homes unless they must," said Humphrey, when they were safely away; "but the fire hath saved us, and I warrant thee we pay not one hundred and fifty gold pieces for the saving neither."

"Didst pay so much?" asked Hugo.

"Yea, lad," answered Humphrey. "It seemeth the 'friend to his counsel' did set the price he was to ask, and nothing less would content him. He did even hint at more."

"And how much remaineth?" asked Hugo.

"But fifty gold pieces, lad. We be now near our journey's end. Mayhap they be enough."

"Yea," replied Hugo, thoughtfully. "I must not go to the priory of the Holy Trinity unless I have great need. So said my uncle to me."

"And where is that, lad?"

"Here in London. It is a powerful and wealthy priory, but my uncle did say it is as well to pass it by if I can."

"Mind thou thine uncle, lad. But whither go we now?"

"To Dover. Then do we take ship to France."

They had now come to the new London bridge which was of stone. Over it they went, and had just started on their journey from its southern end when, in haste, old Bartlemy, clad as the nurse, arrived at the White Horse. He had slowly and laboriously counted his gold pieces three times before it occurred to him that one hundred and fifty of these treasures was no great sum. And that, if he did as Humphrey had requested, he would be able to add other gold pieces to his store. Thus thinking, he had repaired to the hiding-place of his disguise, put it on, and set out.

At the same moment of his arrival the innkeeper came back, and a little later the grooms began to straggle in.

Old Bartlemy, however, paid no attention to who came in or who went out. His sole concern was to find Humphrey. Not succeeding, he appealed to the inn-keeper to know what was become of him.

"Why, that I know not," replied the innkeeper, indifferently. "Most like he hath not yet returned from the fire."

Impatiently old Bartlemy, forgetting that he was a woman, and nurse to a young lady of the better sort, sat down in the inn yard upon a bench. And ever and anon as no Humphrey appeared he got up and mingled with the knots of other men standing about, only to return to his seat. Finally he could restrain himself no longer, but eagerly began to inquire of all newcomers as to the whereabouts of Humphrey. Now while his were questions which no man could answer, they were put in such a manner as to make men stare curiously upon him. For they were such questions as one man would ask of another, and not the timid inquiries of an ignorant old woman. Finally, one of the bystanders more daring than the rest advanced, and boldly turned back the hood of the head-rail, letting it hang down over his shoulders, and the head of an old man was revealed. A murmur of surprise and expectation now ran through the crowd, and the same bold hand bodily removed the head-rail and the robe beneath it; and there stood old Bartlemy in his gray woollen tunic, his legs bare from the knees down, and his feet encased in skin shoes reaching to his ankles.

"Well done, mother!" cried the bold revealer of his identity. "And now do thou tell us speedily who is this esquire Humphrey whom thou seekest. Mayhap he is as little an esquire as thou art an old woman."

Bartlemy looked from face to face, but he answered nothing.

At this moment a groom came running from the stables. "Master! master!" he cried, addressing the innkeeper, "the horse of the esquire Humphrey be gone."

"Gone, sirrah!" repeated the innkeeper. "And whither is he gone?"

"Why, that I know not, master. I only know that the horse of the young lady did bear him company. But the mule of the nurse is still there, wherefore there is no thievery, since he did take but his own."

The bystanders now crowded more closely around Bartlemy, with the innkeeper at the front as questioner.

"Tell us truly, old man," said the innkeeper, threateningly; "who is this esquire Humphrey, and who is the young lady that beareth him company? Make haste with thine answer, or it shall be worse for thee."

"Why," replied old Bartlemy, slowly, as his gaze wandered from face to face, "the esquire is the false priest from Oundle, and the young lady is his novice."

At this reply a man from the rear elbowed his way to the side of the innkeeper. "I know not how it may please thee," he said, "but, on the Watling Street by the meat market two days and more agone, a man with a bailiff to his help did stop a priest and his novice. And he did act like a madman when he did discover that he had stopped the wrong persons, and prated of a reward from the king which he must lose."

Old Bartlemy grinned as he listened. Seeing which the innkeeper pounced upon him. "Were these the priest and his novice?" he asked fiercely.

"Yea, verily," answered old Bartlemy, proudly. "And they would have been caught but for me. And now I know not whither they be gone," he added disconsolately. "And perchance I shall see them no more; nor shall I see the mole on the nose of the good Humphrey more; and so, farewell to the fortune it might bring me."

"And who is the young lady?" said the innkeeper, with a fierce look.

"Why, she be a fine lad," replied old Bartlemy.

The innkeeper reflected amid a low hum of comment.

Then he turned on the man who had told him of the priest and his novice. "Thou sayest the king hath a reward for this priest and his novice?" he asked.

"Yea."

"And who be they?" asked the innkeeper.

"They are like to be as little priest and his novice as they be esquire and young lady. Who be they, I say?"

"I had speech later with the bailiff, and he did say that the priest was a Saxon serving-man, and the novice was the young lord, Josceline De Aldithely, escaping to his father."

"After them! after them!" cried the innkeeper, furiously. "They be a prize!"

In the hurly-burly and din that now arose old Bartlemy slipped out to the stables, got possession of his mule, and rode off unnoticed.

There were in the London of this time many great town houses of the nobles. And that of Lord De Launay was situated in Lombard Street, not far from the White Horse. To it he went riding, at this moment, with a small retinue in livery. He looked in surprise at the commotion before the White Horse, and beckoning a retainer he said, "Find me the meaning of this uproar." Then he rode slowly on to his home.

He had but entered the great square courtyard when the retainer came in on a gallop. "Your lordship, it be this," he said. "They have but just struck the trail of the young Lord De Aldithely and will presently run him to earth, hoping for the reward offered by the king. He rideth now disguised as a lady, and the serving-man rideth as his esquire."

Now Lord De Launay was he who in the guise of a scullion had set Walter Skinner free, and all for the friendship he bore Josceline's father. So calling up twenty of his men-at-arms he sent them in pursuit. "No doubt they ride to Dover," he said. "Make haste to come up with them. Bid the young lord cast aside his woman's garb, and stay ye by them as an escort on the road. Leave them not till they be safely aboard ship and off to France."

The men-at-arms of Lord De Launay were of the best of that time, being both bold and faithful, and their master stood but little in awe of the king. Not that he openly flouted the king's authority, but that, at all times, he dared to pursue the course that seemed to him best. And this he could do for two reasons; he pursued it quietly, and the king felt a little fear of him. Moreover, the king did not discover how much he owed to him for the thwarting of his plans. Else, powerful noble though he was, Lord De Launay would have been punished.

Meanwhile, Hugo and Humphrey were making the best of their way, and stopping not to look to the right hand nor to the left. After them galloped the men-at-arms, and not many miles out of the city they overtook them.

Upon their approach the fugitives gave themselves up as lost. "Lad," said Humphrey, despairingly, "we have done our best, and we be taken at last. No doubt these be the king's men-at-arms that ride so swiftly upon our track. See how they be armed, and how their horses stride!"

Hugo looked over his shoulder, and his face was pale. But there was no regret in his heart for the attempt he had made to save Josceline, even though the king's dungeon seemed now to open before him. He said nothing, and a moment later the men-at-arms swept up and surrounded them, their leader saluting Hugo, much to the boy's surprise. "My lord bids thee cast aside thy woman's dress," said he, "and ride in thine own character."

"And who art thou? And who is thy lord? And wherefore art thou come?" demanded Humphrey, bravely, as he spurred his horse between Hugo and the man-at-arms who had spoken.

The man-at-arms laughed. "I see thou hast cause to dread pursuit," he said. "And, in truth, we did pass some vile knaves riding fast to overtake ye. One and all they do hope for the king's reward, for the old man at the White Horse hath betrayed ye."

Closer to Hugo's side Humphrey reined his horse, and the captain of the men-at-arms laughed louder than before. "Why, what couldst thou do for the lad against us?" he said. "And yet, thou art brave to try. But put away thy fears. Lord De Launay is, as thou shouldst know, the sworn friend of Lord De Aldithely, and he hath sent us to overtake ye and to carry ye safe to the ship at Dover. So let us on and set a merry pace for these knaves that would follow us. But first, off with that woman's robe, my young lord Josceline."

"Willingly!" cried Hugo, who did not even now betray

the secret that he was not Josceline, not knowing what might come of it. And he threw off hood, cloak, and robe while Humphrey looked from the captain to the boy and back again. But without a word to the faithful serving-man, the captain gave the command to the troop, and immediately all were in swift motion.

A mile was left behind them, - two miles, - and now Humphrey looked at Hugo amazed. Among these men-at-arms who treated him with a respect which was like an elixir to him, the boy sat transformed. He held himself proudly, and seemed, as he sat, a part of his horse. His handsome eyes shone, and a genial smile parted his lips.

"Who art thou, dear lad?" thought Humphrey. "And though that I cannot tell, yet this I know, thou art the equal of any De Aldithely." And then Hugo's eyes fell upon him, and they filled with a most kindly light.

Meanwhile the motley crowd that had started in pursuit from the White Horse had become appreciably thinned upon the road. For one was no rider, and was promptly pitched over his horse's head. Another, in his haste, had but imperfectly saddled his horse, so that he was speedily at the side of the road with his horse gone. Others had chosen poor mounts that could go but slowly, being waggoners' horses and not accustomed to any but a slow motion.

All these, with disappointment, saw the hope of the king's reward slipping from them, and looked with envy upon the few who passed them and vanished from their sight, with determination written on their faces. Yet even these were destined to failure and, before Rochester was reached, were fain to turn back, having seen nothing of those whom they sought.

But the troop of men-at-arms with Hugo and Humphrey still sped, halting for the night in a safe spot, and rising betimes in the morning to hurry on, until, their duty done, and the two safely aboard, they turned back at their leisure.

And all this time, upon the sea going down from Scotland was a ship which bore Lady De Aldithely and Josceline. Even in the wilds of Scotland she could not rest, knowing that no spot would remain unsearched if it should be discovered that it was Hugo Aungerville and not Josceline who had fled to France. So she and her son had embarked, and, two days before Hugo and Humphrey, they reached Lord De Aldithely. And there they found William Lorimer and his men-at-arms, but, to Lady De Aldithely's distress, no Hugo nor tidings of him.

"What lad is this thou speakest of?" asked Lord De Aldithely.

And then Lady De Aldithely told him all. "And his name," she ended, "is Hugo Aungerville. Knowest thou aught of him?"

"I should," replied Lord De Aldithely. "Though I have never seen him, I do know he must be the son of my cousin, Eleanor De Aldithely; for he hath her brave spirit, and her husband was Hugo Aungerville. And the lad shall be knighted or ever he arrive. For if he elude the king successfully and on such an errand, risking his own life to save that of another, he hath won his spurs."

Thus it was that when Hugo came welcome was waiting for him in the warm hearts of his kinsfolk. And when he had received his spurs, and Lord De Aldithely asked him what reward he could give him for saving Josceline from the king's hands, the boy smiled archly upon the faithful Humphrey who stood by. "I do ask thee," he said, "that Humphrey may be my esquire."

And from that day Humphrey, a serving-man no longer, followed his dear lad, not only in France, but later in England, when Magna Charta had been signed, and it was safe for them all to return.

Choose from Thousands of 1stWorldLibrary Classics By

Adolphus WilliamWard
Aesop
Agatha Christie
Alexander Aaronsohn
Alexander Kielland
Alexandre Dumas
Alfred Gatty
Alfred Ollivant
Alice Duer Miller
Alice Turner Curtis
Alice Dunbar
Ambrose Bierce
Amelia E. Barr
Andrew Lang
Andrew McFarland Davis
Anna Sewell
Annie Besant
Annie Hamilton Donnell
Annie Payson Call
Anton Chekhov
Arnold Bennett
Arthur Conan Doyle
Arthur Ransome
Atticus
B. M. Bower
Basil King
Bayard Taylor
Ben Macomber
Booth Tarkington
Bram Stoker
C. Collodi
C. E. Orr
C. M. Ingleby
Carolyn Wells
Catherine Parr Traill
Charles A. Eastman
Charles Dickens
Charles Dudley Warner
Charles Farrar Browne
Charles Ives
Charles Kingsley
Charles Lathrop Pack
Charles Whibley
Charles Willing Beale
Charlotte M. Braeme
Charlotte M.Yonge
Clair W. Hayes
Clarence Day Jr.
Clarence E. Mulford

Clemence Housman
Confucius
Cornelis DeWitt Wilcox
Cyril Burleigh
D. H. Lawrence
Daniel Defoe
David Garnett
Don Carlos Janes
Donald Keyhole
Dorothy Kilner
Dougan Clark
E. Nesbit
E.P.Roe
E. Phillips Oppenheim
Edgar Allan Poe
Edgar Rice Burroughs
Edith Wharton
Edward J. O'Biren
John Cournos
Edwin L. Arnold
Eleanor Atkins
Elizabeth Cleghorn
Gaskell
Elizabeth Von Arnim
Ellem Key
Emily Dickinson
Erasmus W. Jones
Ernie Howard Pie
Ethel Turner
Ethel Watts Mumford
Eugenie Foa
Eugene Wood
Evelyn Everett-Green
Everard Cotes
F. J. Cross
Federick Austin Ogg
Ferdinand Ossendowski
Francis Bacon
Francis Darwin
Frances Hodgson Burnett
Frank Gee Patchin
Frank Harris
Frank Jewett Mather
Frank L. Packard
Frederick Trevor Hill
Frederick Winslow Taylor
Friedrich Kerst
Friedrich Nietzsche
Fyodor Dostoyevsky

Gabrielle E. Jackson
Garrett P. Serviss
Gaston Leroux
George Ade
Geroge Bernard Shaw
George Ebers
George Eliot
George MacDonald
George Orwell
George Tucker
George W. Cable
George Wharton James
Gertrude Atherton
Grace E. King
Grant Allen
Guillermo A. Sherwell
Gulielma Zollinger
Gustav Flaubert
H. A. Cody
H. B. Irving
H. G. Wells
H. H. Munro
H. Irving Hancock
H. Rider Haggard
H. W. C. Davis
Hamilton Wright Mabie
Hans Christian Andersen
Harold Avery
Harold McGrath
Harriet Beecher Stowe
Harry Houidini
Helent Hunt Jackson
Helen Nicolay
Hendy David Thoreau
Henrik Ibsen
Henry Adams
Henry Ford
Henry Frost
Henry James
Henry Jones Ford
Henry Seton Merriman
Henry Wadsworth
Longfellow
Henry W Longfellow
Herbert A. Giles
Herbert N. Casson
Herman Hesse
Homer
Honore De Balzac

Horace Walpole
Horatio Alger, Jr.
Howard Pyle
Howard R. Garis
Hugh Lofting
Hugh Walpole
Humphry Ward
Ian Maclaren
Israel Abrahams
J.G.Austin
J. Henri Fabre
J. M. Barrie
J. Macdonald Oxley
J. S. Knowles
J. Storer Clouston
Jack London
Jacob Abbott
James Allen
James Lane Allen
James Andrews
James Baldwin
James DeMille
James Joyce
James Oliver Curwood
James Oppenheim
James Otis
Jane Austen
Jens Peter Jacobsen
Jerome K. Jerome
John Burroughs
John F. Kennedy
John Gay
John Glasworthy
John Habberton
John Joy Bell
John Milton
John Philip Sousa
Jonathan Swift
Joseph Carey
Joseph Conrad
Joseph Jacobs
Julian Hawthrone
Julies Vernes
Justin Huntly McCarthy
Kakuzo Okakura
Kenneth Grahame
Kate Langley Bosher
L. A. Abbot
L. T. Meade
L. Frank Baum
Laura Lee Hope

Laurence Housman
Leo Tolstoy
Leonid Andreyev
Lewis Carroll
Lilian Bell
Lloyd Osbourne
Louis Tracy
Louisa May Alcott
Lucy Fitch Perkins
Lucy Maud Montgomery
Lydia Miller Middleton
Lyndon Orr
M. H. Adams
Margaret E. Sangster
Margaret Vandercook
Maria Edgeworth
Maria Thompson Daviess
Mariano Azuela
Marion Polk Angellotti
Mark Overton
Mark Twain
Mary Austin
Mary Cole
Mary Rowlandson
Mary Wollstonecraft
Shelley
Max Beerbohm
Myra Kelly
Nathaniel Hawthrone
O. F. Walton
Oscar Wilde
Owen Johnson
P.G.Wodehouse
Paul and Mable Thorn
Paul G. Tomlinson
Paul Severing
Peter B. Kyne
Plato
R. Derby Holmes
R. L. Stevenson
Rabindranath Tagore
Rahul Alvares
Ralph Waldo Emmerson
Rene Descartes
Rex E. Beach
Richard Harding Davis
Richard Jefferies
Robert Barr
Robert Frost
Robert Gordon Anderson
Robert L. Drake

Robert Lansing
Robert Michael Ballantyne
Robert W. Chambers
Rosa Nouchette Carey
Ross Kay
Rudyard Kipling
Samuel B. Allison
Samuel Hopkins Adams
Sarah Bernhardt
Selma Lagerlof
Sherwood Anderson
Sigmund Freud
Standish O'Grady
Stanley Weyman
Stella Benson
Stephen Crane
Stewart Edward White
Stijn Streuvels
Swami Abhedananda
Swami Parmananda
T. S. Ackland
The Princess Der Ling
Thomas A. Janvier
Thomas A Kempis
Thomas Anderton
Thomas Bailey Aldrich
Thomas Bulfinch
Thomas De Quincey
Thomas H. Huxley
Thomas Hardy
Thomas More
Thornton W. Burgess
U. S. Grant
Valentine Williams
Victor Appleton
Virginia Woolf
Walter Scott
Washington Irving
Wilbur Lawton
Wilkie Collins
Willa Cather
Willard F. Baker
William Makepeace
Thackeray
William W. Walter
Winston Churchill
Yei Theodora Ozaki
Young E. Allison
Zane Grey

www.ingramcontent.com/pod-product-compliance
Lightning Source LLC
Chambersburg PA
CBHW030124180626
46812CB00002B/543